Landscapes of Language

The Achievement and Context of Richard Brautigan's Fiction

For Judy and Michael

Landscapes of Language:
the Achievement and Context of
Richard Brautigan's Fiction

John Tanner

$\mathcal{HEB}$ ☼ **Humanities-Ebooks**

First published by *Humanities-Ebooks, LLP,*
Tirril Hall, Tirril, Penrith CA10 2JE

The Pdf Ebook is available to private purchasers from http://www.humanities-ebooks.co.uk and to libraries from Ebrary, EBSCO and MyiLibrary.com.

COVER PHOTO: © Erik Weber www.desart.com

ISBN 978-1-84760-242-8 Pdf Ebook
ISBN 978-1-84760-243-5 Paperback
ISBN 978-1-84760-244-2 Kindle Ebook

Contents

General Editors' Introduction

'Contemporary American Literature' aims to highlight the shifts in academic approaches to racial, ethnic and gender issues that have drawn attention to the multitudinous voices constituting what Walt Whitman famously called a 'teeming nation of nations.' At the same time, it offers scholars of American literature an opportunity to re-assess or rediscover authors or texts that have fallen out of fashion, or that never received the critical scrutiny they deserved.

For present purposes, our focus will remain on the literature and literary criticism of the period running from, roughly, the early 1970s to the present. Until then, the literary canon had been constructed around a body of white, largely male, New Yorkers and New Englanders, most notably the figures of F. O. Matthiessen's *American Renaissance* (1941) and Henry James ('The Master'). In the twentieth century the scope widened to include mid-Westerners such as F. Scott Fitzgerald and Ernest Hemingway, and, after the Second World War, Jewish American novelists including Saul Bellow, E. L. Doctorow and Philip Roth, who were placed alongside perpetuators of a more 'traditional' American literature such as John Updike, and the new voices of what would eventually be labelled 'postmodernism,' such as Thomas Pynchon and, slightly later, Don DeLillo. While there is no doubt that nineteenth-century writers—most notably, Whitman, Herman Melville and Mark Twain—had recognised the multicultural possibilities of America, it is the era we are concerned with in this series that changed the way the country viewed and narrated itself in literature, with multicultural fictions that often combined critical and commercial success. Doctorow's *Ragtime* (1975) famously interweaves the stories of three families to rewrite the history and parody the mythology of the United States. The opening pages of the novel rapidly move from a turn-of-the-century world that seems straight out of Henry James or Edith Wharton to a sudden realization of the plurality of American life:

> That was the style, that was the way people lived. Women were
> stouter then. They visited the fleet carrying white parasols.
> Everyone wore white in summer. Tennis racquets were hefty and
> the racquet faces elliptical. There was a lot of sexual fainting.
> There were no Negroes. There were no immigrants.
> ...
> In New York City the papers were full of the shooting of the
> famous architect Stanford White by Harry K. Thaw, eccentric
> scion of a coke and railroad fortune. Harry K. Thaw was the hus-
> band of Evelyn Nesbit, the celebrated beauty who had once been
> Stanford White's mistress. The shooting took place in the roof
> garden of the Madison Square Garden on 26th Street, a spectacu-
> lar block-long building of yellow brick and terra cotta that White
> himself had designed in the Sevillian style. It was the opening
> night of a revue entitled *Mamzelle Champagne*, and as the chorus
> sang and danced the eccentric scion wearing on this summer
> night a straw boater and heavy black coat pulled out a pistol and
> shot the famous architect three times in the head. On the roof.
> There were screams. Evelyn fainted. She had been a well-known
> artist's model at the age of fifteen. Her underclothes were white.
> Her husband habitually whipped her. She happened once to meet
> Emma Goldman, the revolutionary. Goldman lashed her with her
> tongue. Apparently there *were* Negroes. There *were* immigrants.
> (E. L. Doctorow, *Ragtime* [1975])

Among the many strengths of Doctorow's novel is its ability
to highlight the way that an intermingling of disparate voices—
immigrant, African American and 'white'—is at the heart of American
creativity, whilst the book provides constant reminders both of the
power of national mythologies such as Benjamin Franklin's rags
to riches narrative, and of just how hard it is to sustain principled
opposition to this narrative in the face of the financial inducements and
social opportunities offered to a few individuals. The transformation
of the East European immigrant Tateh, defined by his socialism,
devotion to his family and to apparently unshakable faith in core
moral values into the Baron Ashkenazy, creator of movies depicting

an implausibly harmonious (and immensely popular) multi-ethnic gang of American children finally reiterates Doctorow's insistence that history has always been told by the masters, but also his belief that—by 1975—there was the possibility of other histories emerging.

At least within the academic community, Doctorow was probably correct: while studies of Hawthorne, Melville and James most certainly did not disappear, they were joined by a growing corpus of studies that insisted that yes, 'there *were* Negroes [or 'African Americans']. There *were* immigrants.' Studies such as Jane Tompkins's *Sensational Designs* (1986), Michael J. Denning's *Mechanic Accents* (1987) and Russell J. Reising's *The Unusable Past* (1987) assimilated and developed the work of earlier multicultural critics such as Annette Kolodny and Richard Slotkin to challenge the assertions underpinning the construction of the American canon and demand spaces for works by women novelists and the writings of African Americans and immigrants. And while the *literary* value of literature did at times seem to disappear from the interminable canon wars of the 1980s and 1990s (though not in the books cited above), the theoretical battles that quite often really did split departments into highly antagonistic factions in the late twentieth century do seem to have resulted in a twenty-first-century critical culture in which a return to stress on the literariness of literature lives alongside the general embrace of the fact that writing the canon is not the preserve of Ivy League white males.

At the same time as the work of critics such as Tompkins and Reising recovered the long-marginalised presence of writings by women and African Americans, new generations of American writers from a plenitude of ethnic and class positions have assumed pivotal places in contemporary American literature. While there seems to be no doubt that Toni Morrison is the best known—and one of the most highly acclaimed—of these voices, she is but one figure in a literary marketplace that increasingly problematises the notion of what American literature is and the kinds of critical tools required to discuss it in any meaningful fashion. The focus on the 'playful,' experimental postmodernism of the 1960s and 1970s has been replaced by (or, at least, joined by) a return to the search for the *authentic* experience of narratives of migration (both to and from the United States), of the precarious balancing of assimilation to a dominant culture and the desire to retain a culture of one's own, and of the eternal questioning of what it means to be an 'American.' In an increasingly 'globalised' community, these narratives are now as often recounted by writers from North Africa or China as by those from Eastern Europe, but most seem to retain a faith—at some level—in the mythological promises of the United States. To listen to the taxi drivers of Boston, or Austin, or San Francisco, or Denver is to hear life stories—if not quite *novels*—that are at once strikingly different in the details of war zones fled and disillusionment with the 'old' country, and an innate faith in the possibilities of a world still almost as new as that first viewed by Fitzgerald's Dutch sailors at the end of *The Great Gatsby*. And while contemporary American literature is as often marked by a disillusionment with the nation that can be traced through most of the nation's literary history, this is accompanied by the sense of possibility that is heard so often in the voices of 'ordinary' Americans, but also by the recognition that—post-9/11—the United States is as vulnerable to external forces as are the nations left behind.

The enormous diversity of American literatures currently being created ensures that a series called 'Contemporary American Literature' is bound to be both eclectic and inconsistent. There is no longer even the possibility—or the desire—to create a master narrative able to 'contain' (to return once more to Whitman) the multitudinous voices that constitute a 'national' narrative. Indeed, recent approaches to the Trans- or Post-national condition would rightly question the enduring legitimacy of such a concept. This means that the series makes no claims to unfurl organically, beneath any but the broadest of themes. Books studying the emergence and development of particular hyphenated American groups are accompanied by those looking at genre, or at single authors. To study the world we live in requires tools and methodologies that may differ from those used to approach the texts of the past. What unites the books in this series is their contribution to our understanding of the here and now.

Christopher Gair and Aliki Varvogli

Introduction

Before *Trout Fishing in America* was published in 1967, Richard Brautigan had little reputation outside his adopted home of San Francisco. The city's avant-garde arts scene was well established, although probably past its peak, but Brautigan was a relatively minor figure known chiefly for his poetry. *A Confederate General from Big Sur* (1964) had been his first published novel but sold fewer than a thousand copies. *Trout Fishing*, his first-written novel, was rejected by publishers for years, and two subsequent novels, *In Watermelon Sugar* and *The Abortion*, were also rejected. When *Trout Fishing* finally did appear it was an unexpected success, eventually selling more than two million copies. It made Brautigan a celebrity, especially among young adults. This was the year of San Francisco's Summer of Love, when tens of thousands of hippies, would-be hippies and assorted fellow-travellers arrived to sample the Haight-Ashbury neighbourhood's much-publicised menu of peace, love (not to mention sex), flower-power, psychedelic music and psychedelic drugs. *Trout Fishing*, although first drafted in the early Sixties, seemed to encapsulate the counter-cultural flavour of the times.

For several years, Brautigan maintained the impetus provided by *Trout Fishing. Confederate General* became a success and so did the two previously-unpublished novels, *Watermelon* (1968) and *The Abortion* (1971). Fame brought a home in Bolinas, north of San Francisco, and a farmhouse, land and rental properties in Montana. Lawrence Ferlinghetti, the poet-proprietor of San Francisco's famous bookshop and publishing house, City Lights, remembers that Brautigan was the store's most popular author in 1969, outselling other outsider icons such as Allen Ginsberg, Jack Kerouac and William S. Burroughs (Meltzer, *Beat* 75). Gradually, however, although his output of prose and poetry steadily grew, Brautigan's commercial success shrank, and so did critical attention, which had always been divided. His income was alarmingly reduced, he was depressed, divorced for the second time, drinking heavily, and had fallen out with many of his friends. In September, 1984, Brautigan emulated one of his literary heroes, Ernest Hemingway, by killing himself with a shot to the head. He was alone at his home in Bolinas and the remains of his body were not found for several weeks. Brautigan, a master of the surreal, had left a misleadingly routine message for phone callers which itself grew more and more surreal as the machine's batteries ran down and Brautigan's voice slowed and deepened towards a halt (Wright, Abbott *Downstream* 138, Hjortsberg *Jubilee* 7).

Brautigan's suicide did not cause the revival of interest that an author's death sometimes brings and his current ranking in the public consciousness can be measured by comparing the number of returns he receives in a Google internet search with those achieved by the writers he once outsold at City Lights.

Google Search Returns, 12 June, 2012

William Burroughs	15,500,000
Jack Kerouac	9,160,000
Allen Ginsberg	4,420,000
Richard Brautigan	653,000

The main intention of this book is to argue the case for a wider critical acceptance of Brautigan as an important contributor to innovative 20th-century American fiction. I hope the study adds to Brautigan scholarship primarily through the conclusions I draw about the writer's use of language, about his strong sense of books as physical/visual artefacts, and about the nature and achievement of *Trout Fishing*. Many assertions, positive and negative, have been made about Brautigan's work and I have tried to test their validity through detailed textual study and by placing Brautigan within the context of his peers. I focus on the four novels which Brautigan wrote during the 1960s and on the short stories from that period collected in *Revenge of the Lawn*. He made his name in the Sixties and everything that is important, innovative and characteristic in his prose can be found in that decade's output. Seven more books of fiction were published and received with decreasing enthusiasm. I will touch upon them, but little in this later work offers significant changes of style or subject matter. Therefore, by concentrating on the 1960s, I can examine texts with greater thoroughness to provide a more detailed analysis of Brautigan's prose while omitting nothing that would materially alter our perception of it. This strategy also allows space for an extended study of Brautigan's most innovative book, *Trout Fishing*, and for addressing important literary, cultural and biographical contexts which help our understanding of his work. Although this is a study of Brautigan's fiction, I have also found space to write about his poetry of the 1950s and 1960s – not because it helps establish his literary worth (the reverse is true) but because it is crucial to Brautigan's prose. He began as a poet and virtually everything that characterises his prose can be found first in his poetry. He had always wanted to write novels, he says, but "wrote poetry for seven years to learn how to write a sentence" ("Old Lady" 293). The result is hybrid texts in which his nominal prose frequently looks and reads like poetry. Indeed, Michael McClure believes that it is wrong to call Brautigan a novelist; he prefers to see him as the creator of extended prose poems ("Ninety-One Things" 166).

The term "surreal", and its variants, will be found frequently in this study. They have two related meanings: the common usage, which refers to the presentation of phenomena beyond our notions of the rational or "normal", and a more specific reference to the beliefs and artistic practices of the surrealist movement which emerged in the 1920s, with André Breton as its most prominent theorist. The movement privileged the subconscious over the reasoning mind and sought access to the power of the subconscious through the world of dreams, with its dissonant juxtapositions. The context should make it clear which meaning is intended; often both are applicable.

Bracketed references to passages in Brautigan's texts are differentiated from other references by having their page numbers preceded by an abbreviation of the relevant title, as follows: *The Edna Webster Collection of Undiscovered Writings*, UW; *The Pill* versus *the Springhill Mine Disaster*, TP; *Revenge of the Lawn*, RL; *A Confederate General from Big Sur*, CG; *In Watermelon Sugar*, WS; *The Abortion,* TA; *Trout Fishing in America*, TF; *Rommel Drives on Deep into Egypt*, RD; *Willard and his Bowling Trophies*, WB; *June 30th, June 30th*, JJ. Page citations for *Watermelon, The Pill* and *Trout Fishing* refer to the Houghton Mifflin collected edition of the three books, entitled *Richard Brautigan's Trout Fishing in America, The Pill* versus *the Springhill Mine Disaster, and In Watermelon Sugar*. In the list of works cited, the medium is print unless otherwise stated.

The views of Marc Chénetier, Jerome Klinkowitz and Keith Abbott have been particularly important in developing my own approach to Brautigan, as has the stress by Ian Davidson, who supervised my doctoral thesis, on the poetic roots of Brautigan's fiction. I thank Dr. Davidson for his encouragement, and also Christopher Gair and Aliki Varvogli, whose editing and suggestions have made this a better book than the one they received. Finally, this study would barely have been possible without Prof. John F. Barber's astonishing online Brautigan resource at www.Brautigan.net.

Chapter One: In fragments

Growing up poor in the Pacific Northwest; juvenilia; among the literary bohemians of San Francisco

When Brautigan died in 1984 he left behind a continuously revised, incomplete work of fact and/or fiction: the story of his early days in the Pacific Northwest. Brautigan spoke very little about that time, and what he did say often contradicted others or his own previous accounts. For the most part he was silent or vague, as when he refused to tell his daughter, Ianthe, anything about his mother despite repeated requests. He would not even reveal her name (I. Brautigan 3). Finally, when Ianthe was 19, he briefly showed her a picture of his mother before burning it (I. Brautigan 155). The man named by Richard's mother on the birth certificate – her then husband, Bernard Brautigan – has denied paternity, saying that he and his wife had separated several years earlier; a man who was allegedly having an affair with her after the separation is said by Brautigan Snr. to be the real father (Hjortsberg *Jubilee* 23).

Such contradictions, omissions and vagueness have helped make the story of Brautigan's childhood and youth a collection of biographical fragments that resist the construction of a detailed, coherent narrative. The writer Keith Abbott, a friend of Brautigan's in San Francisco, comments:

> The effect was ghostly, as if Brautigan's past had faded into a kind of surrealist museum whose holdings were indicated only by chalk outlines. These outlines gave off the strong suggestion of crime, of accidents and injury. They hinted at painful events and terrors and tortured relationships, but only rarely did Brautigan confirm them, and then often in an abstract way. ("Introd." xiii)

The "chalk outlines" that follow are confirmed by documentary evidence or else by credible testimony.

Richard Gary Brautigan was born in Tacoma, Washington, on Jan 30, 1935, to Lulu Mary Brautigan. Mother and son lived a poor and peripatetic existence in the Northwest. Brautigan acquired a series of "step-fathers", some of whom he accused of physically abusing him (I. Brautigan 89), and three siblings, each with a different father. At one point, it appears that Brautigan's mother left him with one of the surrogate fathers (Wright, I. Brautigan 89). The family eventually settled in Eugene, Oregon, where Brautigan graduated high school, left home, and tried to establish himself as a writer while making a bare living with odd jobs. His mother and the final step-father, William Folston Jnr., neither supported nor understood his ambition, according to Brautigan's half-sister, Barbara (Wright, Barber *Archive*).

These generally-accepted events express a consistent pattern of disruption: Brautigan is born into a broken marriage, is moved from home to home, town to town, school to school, and from step-father to step-father. Even his name is subject to change. He begins high school with the surname "Porterfield" (the name of one of the step-fathers) but before graduating is told by his mother that his "real" name is "Brautigan", which he subsequently uses (Barber *Archive*). His early life, like much of his prose and poetry, is composed of fragments. The culmination comes in December 1955 when Brautigan, aged 20, performs a very literal act of fragmentation by throwing a stone through a glass panel at a police station. He had asked the police to lock him up. They told him that they had no cause, so Brautigan gave them one. He was broke, had developed a hopeless crush on a 14-year-old girl, Linda Webster, had made no real headway with his literary ambitions, and was at odds with his family. Brautigan's own explanation for his action, some years later, is that he was hungry and just wanted the free meals that the jail would offer (I. Brautigan 155). He got them, presumably, but also got something rather less palatable: a court order for assessment at the state asylum, where he remained for almost three months, was given electric shock treatment and diagnosed as a paranoid schizophrenic – a verdict that continued the pattern of disruption/fragmentation, in this case of the mind's powers of perception.

If the diagnosis has any validity, it offers an intriguing perspective on the source of Brautigan's idiosyncratic use of language, disregard for literary conventions, love of the non-sequitur, and habit of presenting the commonplace as surreal and the surreal as commonplace. R. D. Laing, for instance, connects schizophrenic states with the ability to "see through" perceived normality and call it into question. Deleuze and Guattari link schizophrenia not only to a capacity for challenging orthodox perceptions of normality in general but to a specific capacity for challenging literary orthodoxy, producing "a violence against syntax, a concerted destruction of the signifier" (133). Laing, while accepting the existence of delusional states, is concerned about the difficulty of determining whether someone is truly delusional when "all our frames of reference are ambiguous and equivocal" (11). Psychiatry can become an enforcement agency for cultural values, "a technique of brainwashing, of inducing behaviour that is adjusted by (preferably) non-injurious torture" (12). Here he would presumably be thinking of the kind of electric-shock "therapy" applied to Brautigan.

Shortly after his asylum stay, Brautigan left Eugene, cut off contact with his family, and moved to San Francisco via a short spell in Reno, Nevada. He left behind him several notebooks of juvenilia. They were given to Edna Webster, a confidante and the mother of Linda Webster. Much of the material was published, 16 years after Brautigan's death, in *The Edna Webster Collection of Undiscovered Writings*. The contents are a mix of poetry and short prose pieces and the collection is characterised by gaucheness, cliché, banality, posturing and other such embarrassments. This, for example, is how the young Brautigan reflects on warfare:

Called War

I never want
to go away
to a place
called War.

I don't think
you want
to go there either. (UW 113)

Yet no-one should be surprised when juvenilia are juvenile. More telling is the experimental spirit of much of the work, written far from the nurturing avant-garde milieu that Brautigan would find in San Francisco. Many characteristics of his later work can be found here, even if underdeveloped. These include the blurring of distinctions between prose and poetry, a concern for the spatial qualities of text, fragmentation as a strategy with collage as a structuring principle, and an understanding of books as aesthetic artefacts. The latter can be seen in the way Brautigan presented his work. Burton Weiss bought his early notebooks of writings from Edna Webster and was struck by the way in which Brautigan had treated each of them as an individualised art object: "Each notebook is a handmade book, meticulously laid out by the author, with hand-lettered title, dedication page, and chapter heads" ("Introd."). The texts themselves frequently show a heightened awareness of the non-semantic qualities of written language, the way in which it can interact visually with the space surrounding it to influence the way we construct meaning. In "trite story" (68), for instance, the information is parcelled out in terse, phlegmatic sentences, with a layout suggesting poetry not prose; because each fragment is isolated we are forced to concentrate on the parts rather than the whole, absorbing each piece of information before moving on to the next. It is as if we are watching a film in successive freeze-frames. This piece also supports accounts of Brautigan's mother having left him for a time.

I spent a winter in Butte, Montana.

●

That was after my mother had run off with a man named Frank, or Jack.

●

My father was a cook and worked long hours. I seldom saw my father, except when I ate my meals, because he was living with a whore named Virginia.

●

Virginia didn't like me.

●

I had my own hotel room.

This visual presentation was intended to be even more striking. William Hjortsberg points out that the blobs used as dividers here, and in some other pieces in *Undiscovered Writings*, are actually a ruse by the publisher to save space. In Brautigan's manuscript, each fragment appears on a separate page ("Poetic Injustice?").

Poetry, including poetry-prose hybrids, is the heart of the collection and it is clearly far removed from the established aesthetics of the time. The dominant American poetic mode was that of the "well-wrought" verse. It followed the New Critical taste for what Marjorie Perloff defines as the "tightly structured lyric, distinguished by its complex network of symbols, its metaphysical wit, and its adoption of traditional meters" (11). Instead, Brautigan draws on what one might call the alternative canon of American poetry. There are echoes of Emily Dickinson, William Carlos Williams, Robert Creeley, Kenneth Patchen and E. E. Cummings. The minimalist approach employed also recalls the Japanese haiku; Brautigan says that he read and admired translations of the Japanese masters, Bashō and Issa, in his late teens ("Introd." 8 JJ). There is also a strong flavour of the early Hemingway in much of the work, apparent in the short, stabbing sentences of "trite story" (above). Throughout Brautigan's life, however surreal his literary excursions, his basic unit of expression remained the simple, declarative sentence associated with Hemingway.

Brautigan left much of his juvenilia at home, but the principles underpinning it went with him to San Francisco. The city provided Brautigan with a literary education, the encouragement and advice of innovative peers, and a platform for his work. Presumably, San Francisco's post-war reputation for literary innovation drew Brautigan as it had drawn many others. The so-called San Francisco Renaissance encompassed a range of arts but was particularly important in maintaining and developing the alternative literary canon, interacting with like-minded nodes of activity across America. Brautigan would have found a strong artistic community, centred on North Beach, which was characterised by one of its leading figures, Kenneth Rexroth, as expressing "total rejection of the official high-brow culture" ("Disengagement" 15). There were cliques, feuds, and also a number of writers, such as Allen Ginsberg, who found Brautigan's poetry unpalatable (Abbott *Downstream* 36). In turn, Ginsberg's most celebrated work, "Howl", was dismissed by fellow poet Jack Spicer, Brautigan's mentor, as "crap" (Ellingham and Killian 276). Clearly, the bohemian artistic scene was yet another system of fragmentation. Nevertheless, a shared sense of artistic and cultural "outlaw" status was sufficient to make these fragments cohere.

Modernists such as William Carlos Williams were influential and so was surrealism, although Michael Davidson sees the scene as being generally neo-romantic; there was a desire to "enchant, invoke, and inspire" (6). However, as with Frank O'Hara and the so-called New York School poets, there was really no common style, only a shared rejection of establishment modes. O'Hara and James Schuyler, both active in the 1950s, give a flavour of the rebel aesthetics. Schuyler seems to have seen the issue in terms of English cultural imperialism, saying of the conventional "well-wrought" verse that it was produced by and for "campus dry-heads who wishfully descend tum-ti-tumming from Yeats out of Graves with a big kiss for Mother England" (418). O'Hara links loss of faith in religious structures to loss of faith in poetic structures: "I don't believe in God so I don't have to make elaborately sounded structures.... I don't even like rhythm, assonance, all that stuff" ("Personism" 498). In the alternative canon, your poetry could follow the American Dream: it could be anything you wanted it to be.

Brautigan's arrival in San Francisco in 1956 roughly coincided with that of the city's Beat sub-culture. Beat icons such as Ginsberg, Kerouac, Herbert Huncke, and Gregory Corso first met in New York, but as the Beat sensibility became an international cult phenomenon, San Francisco was probably the place most associated with it in the public consciousness. The Beats were iconoclasts who had a shared distaste for materialism and the status-seeking "rat race" of mainstream culture. They also rejected that culture's perceived conservatism and repressiveness towards freedom of speech, artistic expression, drug use, and sexuality. There was no organisation that could be joined, and no manifesto, although Kerouac's episodic novel of bohemian journeying, *On the Road*, acted as an unintended recruiting sergeant and do-it-yourself guide for would-be "Beatniks". Artistic expression was important, broadly speaking in avant-garde modes, and most of the leading Beats were writers. Be-bop and other contemporary jazz forms were prized, reflecting the Beat spirit of spontaneity and self-expression, and there was also, among many prominent Beats, a strong identification with marginalised ethnic groups and with the natural world. A search for spiritual enlightenment characterised leading Beats and often led to involvement with eastern mysticisms such as Zen Buddhism.

With the rise of the Beats a new wave of talent was emerging in the city, including Lawrence Ferlinghetti, Gary Snyder, Philip Whalen, David Meltzer, Michael McClure, Joanne Kyger and, from time to time, Kerouac, Ginsberg and Corso. Most of these have tended to be associated with the Beats, but only Ginsberg, Kerouac and Corso can be confidently labelled as such. Longer-established poets in and around town included Rexroth, William Everson (Brother Antoninus), Philip Lamantia, Robert Duncan, Jack Spicer, and Robin Blaser. The San Francisco writers attended each other's readings, socialised in the same bars, held discussion groups at each other's homes and the homes of patrons, and provided encouragement and criticism.

Brautigan has often been labelled a Beat, or else linked to San Francisco's subsequent counter-cultural wave, the hippies. Like the Beats, the San Francisco hippies rejected mainstream norms but were a generation younger and, broadly speaking, lacked the intellectual and literary concerns of leading Beats. Also, whereas the Beats tended to eschew outward display, the hippies delighted in their flamboyant appearance and gatherings. Ferlinghetti manages to mock both Brautigan and the hippies in a single gibe by saying, "I guess Richard was all the novelist the hippies needed. It was a non-literate age" (Wright). Ginsberg, when asked by a student at UC Berkeley why the hippies did not articulate their views, responded, "'Oh, come on … Because they're *inarticulate*'" (Kramer 83). Each movement was an influence on Brautigan and he shared some attitudes and interests with both groups, at least for a time. But there tended to be a conceptualising and spiritual dimension to the Beats which Brautigan lacked. As for being a hippie, the *Trout Fishing* cover photo of Brautigan – flower shirt, beads, long hair, retro-Western moustache and hat – certainly makes him look the part. Along with some other North Beach "veterans", such as Ginsberg and McClure, he read at hippie events; he was also involved with the Diggers, who gave away food and clothing and tried to promulgate their anti-capitalist, anarchist-tinged ideas among the hippies. However, Abbott says that Brautigan's hippie-like appearance actually predated the hippies (Abbott "In the Riffles" 18) and although the Diggers were active in the hippie community they were not a product of it. Nor does Brautigan seem to have shared the hippies' taste for psychedelic drugs (I. Brautigan 99) and rock music (Abbott *Downstream* 59); he did not fit their age profile, either, because at 32 in 1967, Brautigan was at least a dozen years older than most of San Francisco's hippie migrants. Like his work, Brautigan was his own category.

His core audience, though, came from young people attracted to the spirit of non-conformity which the Beats and hippies represented, and he was particularly popular on college campuses. Indeed, for a time, Brautigan became a media-appointed spokesman for a turbulent generation which was not his own. As Tom Wolfe has noted, the hippies produced little or no literature, to the disappointment of publishers (Wolfe "New Journalism" 45); you might say that Brautigan was willingly co-opted to fill a gap in the market. Many of his readers responded, I suspect, to *Trout Fishing*'s iconic cover photo, in which Brautigan looks part gunslinger, part hippie and part rock star. Inside the covers, *Trout Fishing*'s hip irreverence, subversion of structure, off-beat comedy and surreal juxtapositions caught a particular youth zeitgeist. This was a time when the surreal could be found in popular song lyrics and was fashionable in the names of rock bands (Moby Grape, The Electric Prunes, The Strawberry Alarm Clock etc. could be chapter headings in a Brautigan novel). Tellingly, when first the Beats and then the hippies became unfashionable, Brautigan seemed keen to distance himself from them.[1] Attitudes and causes might come

---

1   For instance, he told Bruce Cook that he had arrived in San Francisco "'after the Beat thing had died down'" (Cook 207); in fact he arrived in the year that "Howl" was published. Abbott says that before *Sombrero Fallout*'s publication in 1976, when hippies were more likely to be mocked than emulated, he and Brautigan rewrote the blurb to remove "1960s hippie buzz words". (*Downstream* 122).

and go, but Brautigan's only lasting attachment was to language and its capacity for imaginative transcendence.

Photographs of Brautigan from the late 1950s and early 1960s show a gangly, rather goofy-looking young man, a farm boy rather than a cult figure.[1] The blond hair is still short, by later standards, and although he has a moustache it is not the extravagant, swaggering growth it would become; instead it just seems to add to the general air of awkwardness. He married Virginia (Ginny) Alder in 1957. They lived in a series of cheap, rented apartments and had a daughter, Ianthe, in 1960. Ianthe's birth, says Abbott, did not stop Brautigan cruising the North Beach literary nightlife, leaving Virginia and child at home, which she resented (*Downstream* 45). Virginia confirms that Brautigan's "socializing" was a problem, but places more stress on heavy drinking which, she says, made him violent and abusive (Anderson). In 1962 they separated. Many other women followed, but Brautigan was never able to establish a stable, long-lasting relationship. His second marriage, to Akiko Yoshimura, whom he met in Japan, ended in separation in 1979 after only two years; an acrimonious divorce followed.

Before the break-up with Virginia, the first draft of *Trout Fishing* was written, or partly written, during a 1961 family trip to the Snake River country of Idaho. Virginia's recollection of Brautigan's writing sessions on that trip emphasises the strong influence of poetry as he tried to construct his first extended fiction:

> "We'd camp beside the streams, and Richard would get out his old portable typewriter and a card table. That's when he began to write *Trout Fishing in America*. He had to learn to write prose; everything he wrote turned into a poem." (Wright)

---

1   For example, I. Brautigan: 7, 18, 131.

Chapter Two: Cultivating the hybrids

Brautigan's San Francisco poetry, 1957–1968; the short stories of
Revenge of the Lawn

The Pill versus *the Springhill Mine Disaster*

There was a cottage-craft feel to the process of publishing Brautigan's
San Francisco poetry, as the artist Kenn Davis remembers from his
involvement with 1958's *The Galilee Hitch-Hiker*. He had been asked
by Brautigan to provide a cover illustration. He produced a drawing,
which Brautigan accepted, but that was not the end of his involvement,
nor of Brautigan's. The nominal publishers were San Francisco's
White Rabbit Press, but they had no binding facilities. The pages and
covers were delivered loose to Brautigan. He and Virginia and Davis
"sat around and needle and threaded the copies together, drinking
wine and yakking" (Davis 66). Only 200 copies were printed, and
one important distribution outlet was the street. Davis recalls selling
copies to tourists one day so that he, Brautigan and Virginia would
have enough money to go to the cinema: " 'Right here,' I'd say, 'this
is the genuine thing. Real Beat poetry. Get it right here'" (66). The
previous year, Brautigan and Virginia, this time joined by the poet
Ron Loewinsohn, a friend of Brautigan, had collated and fixed pages
into black covers for 100 copies of his first book, *The Return of the
Rivers*; they pasted a white label on every front and Brautigan signed
his name on each of them (Barber *Archive*).

This personalisation, attention to the look and feel of the books,
and involvement in their production[2] and distribution, take us back

---

2   With mimeographed poems, Brautigan even became his own typesetter because
    a stencil taken from his typewritten manuscript was used in the printing process;
    in forming Carp Press, the imprint for two of Brautigan's poetry books, he and
    Virginia became co-publishers.

to Brautigan's Eugene notebooks; they create artefacts which resist literary commoditisation and stress the notion of the book as an integrated semantic/visual/physical entity. *Please Plant This Book*, published in 1968, is the most theatrical expression of this. Brautigan prints his poems on seed packets and invites readers to plant them. It is an ingenious idea, as much a conceptual artwork as literature, but the poems themselves are disappointing. They illustrate a trend: Brautigan's later 1960s' verse is more prone to sentimentality, occasional naivety and irritating whimsicality, probably influenced by the peace-love-and-flowers ethos of San Francisco's hippie scene. Apart from the titles already mentioned, Brautigan's poetry publications were *Lay the Marble Tea*, 1959, *The Octopus Frontier*, 1960, and *All Watched Over by Machines of Loving Grace*, 1967. Almost all the poetry in Brautigan's first five books appears in the 1968 volume, *The Pill* versus *the Springhill Mine Disaster*, along with previously-uncollected verse. This compilation is the basis for my discussion of Brautigan's poetry.

The aesthetic of fragmentation is central to Brautigan's verse. You find it in *Hitch-Hiker*'s use of narrative fragments bound together by collage, in the way in which seemingly incompatible images collide in similes and metaphors, in the shattering of meaning that these juxtapositions can create, and in the brevity of many of the poems. *Hitch-Hiker* (TP 52–60) is a series of scenes or short narratives in free verse on the theme of transformation through the creative imagination, using a fictionalised Charles Baudelaire as its central character. This interest in collecting fragments into conceptual, collage-like relationships builds on experiments in Eugene and has parallels in two serial poems by Brautigan's mentor, Spicer: *After Lorca*, which also takes a poet as its focus, appeared the year before *Hitch-Hiker*, and "Billy the Kid" appeared in the same year as Brautigan's poem.

Spicer can also be suggested as an influence on Brautigan's use of the surreal, as can Dada, the surrealists themselves, of course, and Kenneth Patchen's cult novel, *The Journey of Albion Moonlight*, which gets an admiring mention in *Confederate General*; there are parallels, too, in some of the more striking images of Gregory Corso – for example, "a madness of coughing bicycles" (Corso "Vision of

Rotterdam" 18). In Eugene, there are only occasional surreal touches, and they tend to be a dark presence whereas in San Francisco the surreal becomes more central and, often, more playful. This echoes Spicer's own playfulness in, for instance, "Billy the Kid". Spicer develops the conceit that the poem is a hideout for Billy, somewhere he can go "with a sheriff's posse after him," a place where "Billy the Kid can hide when he shoots people" (79). This notion of the creative mind being able to establish its own reality is strongly present in *Hitch-Hiker* and would become important in the prose. It had been expressed as a belief in some of Brautigan's Eugene poetry, but *Hitch-Hiker* exemplifies that power rather than merely stating its existence. Brautigan transcends by juxtaposing seemingly contradictory elements: Jesus as a hitch-hiker, Baudelaire as a fly-drive tourist in Roman-occupied Palestine, or as a psychiatrist in a Californian asylum, or as a fast-food concessionaire in San Francisco who hands out flowerburgers instead of hamburgers (presumably an allusion to Baudelaire's *The Flowers of Evil*). Details of simile and metaphor are constructed in the same way, with dissonant images forced into juxtaposition: Baudelaire's watch is "a twenty-one / jewel Siamese / cat...." that he wears on a gold chain; the insane asylum "rubbed itself / up against his / leg like a / strange cat" (TP 56, 59).

These surreal events and comparisons act as a fragmenting force, disrupting our sense of what is real and making us struggle to construct meaning. In some cases, Brautigan produces metaphors and similes which refuse to allow their twin terms to be fused into a single image, a coherent sense of a perceived world beyond the text. These are what I term his self-subverting metaphors, because instead of heightening our perception of the extra-textual, which is the expected role of metaphoric language, they subvert it. This device becomes even more important in Brautigan's prose. *Hitch-Hiker*'s previously-mentioned comparison of Baudelaire's watch to "a twenty-one/jewel Siamese/cat..." is an example of the technique, as is the poem "Kafka's Hat" (TP 89):

> With the rain falling
> surgically against the roof,
> I ate a dish of ice cream

that looked like Kafka's hat.

It was a dish of ice cream
tasting like an operating table
with the patient staring
up at the ceiling.

Ice cream, operating tables, Kafka's hat, staring patients...it is not possible to integrate these elements into a single image. There is a synthesis in the "surgical" rain and the operating table with its patient, but what have these to do with the taste of the ice-cream or with Kafka's hat? Metaphoric language is being used not to strengthen a connection to the perceived world but to disrupt or deny that connection. Edward Halsey Foster says that Brautigan's metaphors seem to be "caught in a perpetual process of simultaneous creation and dissolution of sense" (21). Jerome Klinkowitz says that their "fiercely independent components keep Brautigan's images from running off as references to the real world; their independent objectiveness keeps them riveted to the page as proof of the artist's act in joining them" (*American 1960s* 44).

Thomas Hearron identifies a further way in which Brautigan uses metaphoric diction to transform and transcend: he allows similes to morph into actuality, another tendency which transfers to his fiction (26). It is a device which Terence Malley also notes, one in which "wildly incongruous analogies are transmuted into identities to striking effect" (32). "Sonnet" (TP 74) is an example:

The sea is like
an old nature poet
who died of a
heart attack in a
public latrine.
His ghost still
haunts the urinals.
At night he can
be heard walking
around barefooted

in the dark.
Somebody stole
his shoes.

The hypothetical poet, initially introduced only for comparative purposes, becomes the focus of the poem; a comparative term is the new
reality.

Through his various metaphoric strategies, Brautigan can render
the everyday as fantastical and the fantastical as utterly normal. This
places him in the role of poet-as-stranger, someone with an outsider's
perspective on the world. The performance of that role can also be
seen in Brautigan's recurring focus on the seemingly trivial, as here:

November 3

I'm sitting in a cafe,
drinking a Coke.

A fly is sleeping
on a paper napkin.

I have to wake him up,
so I can wipe my glasses.

There's a pretty girl
I want to look at.

A strategy of estrangement is much easier to adopt, of course, if you
are already something of a stranger. This was certainly Brautigan's
position in Eugene, and although bohemian North Beach was a
community where outsiders could be insiders, all would be aware
of their separation from the surrounding mainstream world, one in
which many of them, Brautigan included, had to make a living from
time to time. It is also worth recalling the comments of Laing and
those of Deleuze and Guattari, both cited in the previous chapter,
concerning the unorthodox viewpoint to be expected from a schizophrenic (always assuming the validity of Brautigan's diagnosis). Yet
whatever the derivation of Brautigan's estranged and estranging literary persona, what it offers is an ability to see the world freshly.

Ferlinghetti (Wright) and others have characterised this as naivety, but although naïve, hippie-influenced poems can be found they are not typical. The poet-as-stranger perspective comes not from naivety but because Brautigan gives the familiar his full and wondering attention. By being sensitised to what others have stopped noticing, or else have decided is beneath consideration, he is following an American tradition which runs from at least as far back as Thoreau via the likes of Whitman and William Carlos Williams to contemporaries such as Frank O'Hara. Tony Tanner's description of Whitman's poetic method catches the essence of the poet-as-stranger. He says that Whitman "tried to see what America was by looking around him as though for the first time"; he was someone who made "a gesture of passionate attention towards vast stretches of ignored reality" (*Reign* 86). Robert Kern links Brautigan to Williams for this close, neutral attention to objects, and to Pound and the haiku as well. The impersonal voicing can be seen as another debt to Hemingway, and it is an important element in strengthening a sense of estrangement. Its distancing effect also helps to keep sentimentality at bay, as does a playfully self-deprecating mode which emerges post-Eugene. The more Brautigan engages emotionally, the more likely we are to find sentimentality and naivety.

Brautigan's poetry in *The Pill* is not only a celebration of the uncelebrated but also an exercise in extreme brevity. Like O'Hara, Brautigan notes what is around him and what he is thinking or doing without imposing hierarchies of significance; but whereas in O'Hara the effect is that of a panning CCTV camera, a Brautigan poem frequently gives us only a single frame. Sometimes it is something observed, sometimes an emotion felt, sometimes a quick thought or an ingenious comparison. Three examples follow (TP 100, 23, 107), starting with the title poem:

The Pill *versus* the Springhill Mine Disaster

When you take your pill
it's like a mine disaster.
I think of all the people
lost inside of you.

At the California Institute of Technology

I don't care how God-damn smart
these guys are: I'm bored.

It's been raining like hell all day long
and there's nothing to do.

In a Cafe

I watched a man in a cafe fold a slice of bread
as if he were folding a birth certificate or looking
at the photograph of a dead lover.

These terse observations or fragments of experience seem more
appropriate to elements of the Japanese literary tradition than to
western aesthetics.[1] The haiku was well known in the west, particularly
among writers from the alternative canon; Pound had been a notable
experimenter with it and Rexroth produced well-received books of
Japanese poetry in translation.[2] One of the most famous Japanese
poets is Matsuo Bashō (1644–94), and what follows is an example of
his haiku style:

The old-lady cherry
Is blossoming, a remembrance
Of years ago. (Ueda 38)

To most western tastes, this might seem an inadequate performance;
it lacks the concentrated power that we tend to expect from such a
brief verse, particularly as translation and our lack of familiarity with
Japanese literature rob it of the graphic qualities, allusiveness and
associative meanings which are important in the haiku. Cid Corman
and Kamaike Susumu, who translated Basho's *Back Roads to Far
Towns* into English, were obviously aware that a western audience
might expect something meatier in its poetry and so provide a sort
of reader-beware explanatory note, arguing that what is left out by
Bashō is as important as what is included, and adding:

---

1   Brautigan's writing became very popular in Japan and remained so as his popu-
    larity and reputation declined in America. He made many visits there.
2   For example, Rexroth's *One Hundred Poems from the Japanese*.

If, at times, the poems seem slight, remember that mere pro-
fusion, words piled up "about" event, often give an illusion of
importance and scale belied by the modest proportions of human
destiny. (8)

"Slight" would certainly be one of several derogatory words that
might be used to describe Brautigan's "At the California Institute of
Technology" (above) and many other poems in *The Pill*. But within
the aesthetic proposed by Corman and Susumu, Brautigan's brief
observations can seem more acceptable – particularly if we see his
fragments as part of a whole. While he was writing *After Lorca*, Jack
Spicer came to believe that all books of poetry should be treated, like
novels, as a single creative expression. An individual poem might
seem inadequate but that did not matter because it should not be seen
in isolation. In a letter to Robin Blaser, in *Admonitions* (55–65), he
argues:

> Poems should echo and reecho against each other. They should
> create resonances. They cannot live alone any more than we can. (61)

By treating the fragments as part of a greater whole, "inconsequential
things can combine together to become a consequence" (61). *Back
Roads* was certainly intended to be read this way. The aggregate of
its fragments is a picture of what it felt like for Bashō to travel the
countryside of 17th-century Japan; from *The Pill* we experience what
it was like for Richard Brautigan to journey through bohemian San
Francisco in the 1950s–1960s.

One source of inspiration for such fragments was *The Greek
Anthology*, a collection of ancient Greek pieces that includes
incomplete, enigmatic statements. In *Willard and his Bowling
Trophies*, Brautigan transfers his passion for the anthology to one
of the main characters, Bob, who quotes obsessively from the work:

> "These are just fragments. Lines," he said. "Parts of lines
> and sometimes only single words that remain from the original
> poems written by the Greeks thousands of years ago."
> "'More beautiful,'" Bob said. "That's all that's left of a poem."
> "'Having fled,'" Bob said. "That's all that's left of another
> one."

"'He cheats you,'" Bob said. "'Breaking.' 'You have made
me forget all my sorrows.' There are three more." (WB 18)

These quotations certainly support Corman and Susumu's notion that
what is omitted can be as important as what is said. A sense of mysterious absence lends potency to the fragments. Through his use of
the surreal, and through the enigmatic snapshot quality of some of
his briefer verse, Brautigan can conjure something similar. Yet even
enthusiasts of Brautigan tend to be apologetic, or at least equivocal,
about his verse. One can place it in the context of Japanese aesthetics, as I have done, but unless one is steeped in that kind of tradition,
it is hard to avoid concluding that much of Brautigan's verse is slight
and too slackly executed. Although a bold and idiosyncratic poetic
sensibility is at work, it finds its best expression not through poetry
but through prose.

Revenge of the Lawn

Most of the short stories in *Revenge of the Lawn: Stories 1962–1970*
were written during the same period as the later poetry in *The Pill,*
and the overlap between the two is more than chronological; just as
The Pill often seems to be prose cut into short lines, so *Revenge* frequently has the look and feel of poetry. This is a result of the metaphoric language used by Brautigan, his sense of linguistic rhythms,
the extreme brevity of many stories, and the use of non-narrative sub-
jects that are more associated with lyric poetry. All of these qualities
can be seen in "Lint", quoted here in full:

> I'm haunted a little this evening by feelings that have no vocab-
> ulary and events that should be explained in dimensions of lint
> rather than words.
>   I've been examining half-scraps of my childhood. They are
> pieces of distant life that have no form or meaning. They are
> things that just happened like lint. (RL 101)

This is one of the more extreme examples of brevity, but another
story, "The Scarlatti Tilt" (RL 37), is even shorter and 17 pieces take
up only a page or less while another 18 require only two pages. There

are parallels with the italicised vignettes with which Hemingway punctuates his book of short stories, *In Our Time*; but there the pieces can be seen as complementing the main text, whereas here they *are* the text.

For the most part, the concerns and literary characteristics of the poetry are also those of the prose. There are some differences of tone and content but, in general, *Revenge* and *The Pill* are best viewed as a continuum, a single work released in two volumes. They each blur the boundaries between prose and poetry, can be playful, often seek imaginative transcendence of perceived reality, defamiliarise the everyday, commonly prefer fragmentation to cohesive and closed narrative, fuse minimalism with the metaphorical exuberance of surrealism, and struggle with the choice between stoical or amused/ ironic detachment on the one hand and sentimentalised engagement on the other. Despite the uneven quality of *Revenge* – another characteristic shared with *The Pill* – it has many stories of real and neglected achievement.

One of these is "The Weather in San Francisco" (RL 31–32), which relies on Brautigan's ability to subvert our notions of rationality. He creates a world in which the non-sequitur and the fantastical reign and yet relates events as if they are completely unexceptional. The story begins with a "very old woman" asking a butcher for a pound of liver. The narrator immediately, and unaccountably, suggests that this is a strange purchase. He speculates: "Perhaps she used it for a bee hive and she had five hundred golden bees at home waiting for the meat, their bodies stuffed with honey" (RL 31). The butcher does not want to sell her the liver, although his argument in favour of hamburger mince is as odd as the narrator's remarks: "'Look outside. It's cloudy. Some of those clouds have rain in them. I'd get the hamburger,' he said" (RL 31). The woman's only objection to the butcher's logic is that the day will be sunny and therefore liver is appropriate. The butcher sells her the meat, even though he is "stunned" by her choice and "didn't want to talk to her any more"; selling liver to old women "made him very nervous" (RL 31). The woman carries the meat home, and by this time the reader may have forgotten the narrator's bizarre speculation about the "five hundred golden bees" that the woman might have. But just as Brautigan can convert a surreal metaphoric term into the actual, so can he convert a surreal speculation into a perceived reality. The woman walks down a hallway into a room that is full of bees:

> There were bees everywhere in the room. Bees on the chairs. Bees on the photograph of her dead parents. Bees on the curtains. Bees on an ancient radio that once listened to the 1930s. Bees on her comb and brush. (RL 32)

The bees "gather about her lovingly" as she unwraps the liver, so perhaps it actually is their hive. The woman's seemingly bizarre discussion with the butcher about the likelihood of sunshine also achieves unexpected relevance – although it takes another inexplicable occurrence for the relevance to become clear. The woman has a silver platter which, like the weather, is said to be cloudy; soon after the liver is placed upon it, the platter metamorphoses "into a sunny day." A happy ending, therefore, but one that cannot dispel the overall ambience of unease created by Brautigan's construction of a world in which the rational and the expected can no longer be relied upon.

As in his poetry, Brautigan's reconfiguration of our perceived world in "The Weather" seems to have no "message". But there are stories in *Revenge* where a new reality is created in order to comment on the old. This happens, for instance, in "The Wild Birds of Heaven" (RL 39–41). An office worker is nagged by his wife and children into buying a TV that he cannot afford. He walks into a department store, chooses a TV, and tells a female assistant that his credit must be good because " 'I'm already 25,000 dollars in debt' " (RL 39). The assistant is "like a composite of all the beautiful girls you see in all the cigarette advertisements and on television" (RL 39). As a well-trained consumer, the man automatically lights a cigarette. The girl points him towards a door, and from now on the story twists into the surreal. The narrator tells us that the door has a grain "like the cracks of an earthquake" (RL 40) and the cracks are filled with light. He goes on:

> The doorknob was pure silver. It was the door that Mr. Henly had always wanted to open. His hand had dreamt its shape while

> millions of years had passed in the sea.
>   Above the door was a sign:
>   BLACKSMITH.
>   He opened the door and went inside and there was a man wait-
> ing for him. The man said, "Take off your shoes, please."
>   "I just want to sign the papers," Mr Henly said. "I've got a
> steady job. I'll pay on time." (RL 40)

But the man politely insists and tells Mr. Henly to take off his socks,
too. He also wants to know Mr. Henly's height: 5ft 11 inches.

> The man walked over to a filing cabinet and pulled out the
> drawer that had 5–11 printed on it. The man took out a plastic
> bag and then closed the drawer. Mr. Henly thought of a good
> joke to tell the man but then immediately forgot it.
>   The man opened the bag and took out the shadow of an
> immense bird. He unfolded the shadow as if it were a pair of
> pants.
>   "What's that?"
>   "It's the shadow of a bird," the man said and walked over to
> where Mr. Henly was sitting and laid the shadow on the floor
> beside his feet. (RL 40–41)

Then the man removes Mr. Henly's own shadow and nails the shadow
of the bird to his feet. Mr. Henly is neither astounded nor frightened,
merely "a little curious", and grateful that the process is painless (RL
41). The man tells him that he can have his own shadow back in 24
months when he finishes paying for the TV. Of the bird shadow, he
says: "It looks pretty good on you" (RL 41). The female assistant also
seems to approve. Passing her on his way out, Mr. Henly again automatically reaches for a cigarette, but the packet is empty. The story
ends: "The girl stared at him as if he were a small child that had done
something wrong."

The tale is a moral fable in which the often-unacknowledged
bizarreness of desperate, knee-jerk consumerism is made apparent
through the introduction of an event whose bizarre nature is clear.
Mr. Henly's debt is a monstrous shadow from which he cannot be
freed, other than by two years of tribute payments to appease the
shadow of the wild bird – a creature which, by its size, must be a

bird of prey. In return he receives a TV whose advertising will try to bully, shame or seduce him into acquiring even more monstrous shadows. The fact that the shadow is nailed into place recalls the nailing of Christ to the cross. Jesus is said to have died for our sins, and Mr. Henly's symbolic crucifixion can be seen as undertaken on behalf of consumer society – except that there is no suggestion that it will bring salvation. The trading of Mr. Henly's shadow for the wild bird's has another parallel in Christian tradition: it can be read as a Faustian pact in which his own soul/ethical self is traded to the devil of consumerism.

Symbolic use of the surreal as a means of social commentary can also be found in the excellent "Homage to the San Francisco YMCA" (RL 47–49). An un-named man, living on a sizeable pension in a wealthy San Francisco neighbourhood, has a taste for fine poetry and expresses his belief in its powers in a rather unusual way:

> One day he decided that his liking for poetry could not be fully expressed in just reading poetry or listening to poets reading on phonograph records. He decided to take the plumbing out of his house and completely replace it with poetry, and so he did.
>
> He turned off the water and took out the pipes and put in John Donne to replace them. The pipes did not look too happy. He took out his bathtub and put in William Shakespeare. The bathtub did not know what was happening.
>
> He took out his kitchen sink and put in Emily Dickinson. The kitchen sink could only stare back in wonder. He took out his bathroom sink and put in Vladimir Mayakovsky. The bathroom sink, even though the water was off, broke out into tears.
>
> He took out his hot water heater and put in Michael McClure's poetry. The hot water heater could barely contain its sanity. Finally he took out his toilet and put in the minor poets. The toilet planned on leaving the country. (RL 47–48)

The man then tries to put the newly-installed poets and their works to use. "He tried to wash some plates in 'I taste a liquor never brewed' and found there was quite a difference between that liquid and a kitchen sink" (RL 48). He tries to use the lavatory, but the minor poets "began gossiping about their careers as he sat there trying to take a shit" (RL 48). Frustrated, the man decides to get his old plumbing back and berates the poets and their verses for their inadequacy (RL 49). But the poets and poems like the new arrangements. Emily Dickinson's poetry, for instance, informs the man: " 'I look great as a kitchen sink'"; the minor poets think that they " 'look wonderful as a toilet'" (RL 49). Poets and poetry refuse to leave, and throw the man down the stairs.

> That was two years ago. The man is now living in the YMCA in San Francisco and loves it. He spends more time in the bathroom than everybody else. He goes in there at night and talks to himself with the light out. (RL 49)

As Ronald Dietrich and others point out, the tale is a commentary on America's degraded values, in which pragmatic, material worth is the measure of everything. The protagonist certainly believes that literature is worthwhile, but that leads him to assume that there must be some "practical" use for it. His move to the YMCA is symbolic because the institution is representative of religion's accommodation with materialistic values: although the YMCA has Christian roots it is now a place where physical exercise is more important than the exercise of faith.

Such departures from the role of neutral observer/recorder are unusual for Brautigan but can also be found in stories which draw on his problematic childhood in the Pacific Northwest. In these, we can find the role of poet-as-stranger darkening into expressions of alienation. In the poetry, which mostly draws on his San Francisco experiences, Brautigan's childhood has little obvious presence. But *Revenge* offers plentiful versions of it and, with other sombre-toned pieces, these generate a mood of melancholy and loss that the book's comic turns, surreal "trips" and linguistic playfulness can never quite banish. Sara Blackburn says that Brautigan is writing about "how it feels to be alone in America," whether as a child or in one's adult roles. Malley points to loneliness and an identification with losers as recurring motifs (38). Certainly the kind of insouciant response to misfortune found in *The Pill* is absent in Northwest tales such as "Corporal" (RL 99–100). In this, the narrator recalls his childhood in Tacoma in World War II when his school had a drive to collect waste paper; the children are rewarded with military ranks depending on the amount of paper they collect. Because the narrator's family is poor, they do not have much waste paper and neither do they have a car to drive the boy to more affluent neighbourhoods. Hence, while other children rise swiftly to officer rank, the narrator only collects enough to become a corporal. The stripes for this achievement he hides in shame.

Such material risks mawkishness and self-pity unless handled crisply or told as a comic tale against oneself, in the self-deprecating manner of some of *The Pill*'s verses. But although the tone is mostly muted, the final, passionate paragraphs throw all distancing aside to provide an untypically emotional passage:

> The kids who wore the best clothes and had a lot of spending money and got to eat hot lunch every day were already generals. They had known where there were a lot of magazines and their parents had cars. They strutted military airs around the play-ground and on their way home from school.
>
> Shortly after that, like the next day, I brought a halt to my glorious military career and entered into the disenchanted paper shadows of America where failure is a bounced cheque or a bad report card or a letter ending a love affair and all the words that hurt people when they read them.

It can be argued that a passionate denunciation of the way in which privilege begets privilege is no bad thing. However, although the narrator is fully engaged with his own experiences and responses, he disconnects too easily from those of the supposedly more fortunate children. The narrator assumes that they will be exempt from entering the paper shadows, when there is no reason to believe that they will not suffer bad grades and romantic rejection, nor that the odd bounced cheque – or a whole avalanche of them – might not come their way. Also worth noting in this passage is the role played by texts in determining our experience of the world. Texts collected or received are the "paper shadows" that engulf the narrator.

When Brautigan avoids such deep engagement – which is most of the time – he is capable of prose whose unemotional economy is a perfect setting for extravagant similes and metaphors. They are splashes of colour on a neutral background, as here in this extract from "The Post Offices of Eastern Oregon" (RL 72–78), where a terse account of the everyday culminates in an image like something from a Salvador Dali painting:

> An old man came in. He said he wanted a glass of milk. The waitress got one for him. He drank it and put a nickel in a slot machine on his way out. Then he shook his head.
>
> After we finished eating, Uncle Jarv had to go over to the post office and send a postcard. We walked over there and it was just a small building, more like a shack than anything else. We opened the screen door and went in.
>
> There was a lot of post office stuff: a counter and an old clock with a long drooping hand like a moustache under the sea, swinging softly back and forth, keeping time with time. (RL 76)

As in the poetry, some of the short stories show an intense, almost mesmeric focus on brief fragments of seemingly trivial experience. "September California" (RL 113) is typical. It has less than a page of text about two unrelated and unremarkable phenomena: a young woman on a beach and a ship visible beyond her. The only connection between them is their presence in the narrator's consciousness as he surveys or imagines a scene. By being isolated and juxtaposed in this way, they resonate and gain significance.

> 22 September means that she is lying on the beach in a black bathing suit and she is very carefully taking her own temperature.
>
> She is beautiful: long and white and obviously a secretary from Montgomery Street who went to San Jose State College for three years and this is not the first time that she has taken her own temperature in a black bathing suit at the beach.
>
> She seems to be enjoying herself and I cannot take my eyes off her. Beyond the thermometer is a ship passing out of San Francisco Bay, bound for cities on the other side of the world, those places.
>
> Her hair is the same colour as the ship. I can almost see the captain. He is saying something to one of the crew.
>
> Now she takes the thermometer out of her mouth, looks at it, smiles, everything is all right, and puts it away in a little lilac

carrying-case.

The sailor does not understand what the captain said, so the captain has to repeat it.

This pared-down scene, ship and woman, is not only brought into sharp focus but given a tinge of longing. The woman seems to be an object of desire while the ship is bound for places made exotic and desirable by distance and because we cannot know their names or nature. The scene is also invested with a sense of strangeness and unease through a strategy of omission. So many questions are left unanswered. Why is the woman taking her temperature? Why does the narrator believe that she has done this before? Does he know her? Is this a scene observed or imagined? How can her occupation and educational history be known? Even the matter of her hair colour raises a question, creates an awareness of absence and adds to the sense of strangeness. Its description as being "the same colour as the ship" seems reasonable enough; but then we realise that the ship's colour has not been given and that the comparison made is therefore between two absences. The conversation on the ship also takes place in an absence, because the narrator can neither see nor hear what is happening on board. Brautigan is employing a related technique to his actualisation of metaphoric terms. In these, the comparative term becomes an imagined reality. Here, he begins by telling us that the captain is too far away to be seen, then proceeds to an imagined reality in which the captain's conversation can be overheard. The content of that conversation adds a final twist of anxiety. How important are the captain's instructions? Will the crewman understand them when repeated and, if not, will there be tragic consequences?

The familiar is also made strange by the strangeness of Brautigan's comparisons, as in the extract from "Post Offices", above, and this is yet another trait carried through from his poetry. "Pale Marble Movie" (RL 79) provides a striking example. The story is no more than the narrator's recollection of his girlfriend getting out of bed while still not fully awake, being urged by the narrator to get back in, and subsequently doing as he suggests. The setting, we are told in the first paragraph, is a room with a marble fireplace. "Marble" is a favourite Brautigan word and one often used by him in metaphors and similes.

It comes freighted with associations of death and monumental fixity but here, in a return to the word in the final sentence, he releases that weight with a simile whose mysteriousness helps establish the power exercised over the narrator by the seemingly trivial scene: "I have been thinking about this simple event for years now. It stays with me and repeats itself over and over again like a pale marble movie."

It must be admitted that some Brautigan stories, again like his verse, make trivial events seem even more trivial. Nevertheless, there is much to applaud in *Revenge*. The sentimentality that mars *The Pill* is avoided, unless self-pity is deemed sentimental, and many of these pieces resonate through their idiosyncratic synthesis of a poetic sensibility, minimalism, the surreal, disengagement and intense focus, as well as through their startling concision. Malley says Brautigan is "a master of the short short story" (63). Christopher Gair uses analyses of two of them, "The Scarlatti Tilt" and "A Short Story About Contemporary Life in California", to illustrate how Brautigan's fiction simultaneously "draws upon and reconfigures the American canon" ("Perhaps the Words" 12). Many of these stories fully justify such admiring critical attention, and deserve much more of it.

Chapter Three: Things fall apart

A Confederate General from Big Sur

The dominant narrative theme in *Confederate General* is expressed in its opening heading, "Attrition's Old Sweet Song", which is an ironic adaptation of the song title, "Love's Old Sweet Song".[1] The immediate reference is to the American Civil War, but a wider resonance is intended. There is the attrition faced by those such as *Confederate General*'s severely damaged entrepreneur, Johnston Wade, who finds that America's capitalist-consumerist culture can literally drive you mad and make you yearn for bohemian rhapsodies. Then we have the narrator, Jesse, and his eccentric friend, Lee Mellon; they represent Wade's perception of a carefree bohemian life, but Jesse is anything but carefree, and he and Lee have their own war of attrition against poverty and the wilds of California's Big Sur. Finally, there is the much more profound attrition of mortality and the need for ways to protect oneself against its fears and pains. Jesse seems unable to find a satisfactory defence; Lee succeeds by imagining himself in a better life than the one he has. However, this theme from within the narrative is ultimately less important than the mode of that narrative. *Confederate General* is a metafictional text which stresses its own artificiality and its status within a universe of texts and textual conventions. The dominant landscape here is not Big Sur but a landscape of language.

    Confederate General opens with a prologue consisting of two lists, presented as if culled from another text (which may be the case) and therefore continuing the pattern of intertextuality begun by the opening heading. The first list documents the ways in which 126

---

1   James L. Malloy, music, J. Clifton Bingham, words. *Love's Old Sweet Song*. 1884.

Confederate generals failed to complete their wartime commissions (CG 3). The second gives the pre-war professions of these and other generals (CG 4). The lists are succinct expressions of attrition and are followed by an opening chapter which is mostly about the Civil War's Battle of the Wilderness. The sombre facts of this encounter are mixed with humorous fantasy as Brautigan introduces the notion that a tribe of Native Americans from California fought on the Confederate side as the 8th Big Sur Volunteer Heavy Root Eaters. That and the prologue, not to mention the book's title, produce two expectations: this will be a novel about the civil war, and it will mingle tragic historical fact with comic fiction. Only the second expectation is fully met, however, because a contemporary story of urban and pastoral escapades becomes the main focus, slyly introduced by what seems to be a digression from what the narrator terms "this military narrative" (CG 10). The hero/anti-hero is Lee Mellon, a rollicking fantasist who lives by scrounging and occasional theft. Lee tells Jesse that his great grandfather was a Confederate general who fought in the Battle of the Wilderness. A reference book has no mention of him, but Lee continues to believe in his existence and Jesse promises to do the same. Lee, like the narrative, does not want to be constrained by "facts". Jesse calls Lee's capacity for imagining his life into existence a "wonderful sense of distortion" (CG 70).

Lee has been living in an abandoned house in the San Francisco Bay area, where he has been making "a daring cavalry attack" (CG 34) on the gas company by tapping into their supply for free; he leaves to stay at a friend's property at Big Sur, on the Californian coast south of Monterey. He appeals to Jesse to join him in letters suggesting that a pastoral idyll awaits. When his girlfriend leaves him, Jessie quits San Francisco to join Lee, but finds that the promised paradise is a dangerously ramshackle cliff-side cabin with one wall missing; there is a chronic lack of food and a pond full of loud frogs that stop the two impoverished city refugees from sleeping. Some financial relief comes when two teenage boys try to steal petrol from Lee's decrepit truck. Lee lets them go in exchange for all their money: "about $6.72" (CG 67). Lee and Jesse head for Monterey on the proceeds and return with a girlfriend for Jesse, Elaine, whose money allows them to stock up with supplies including, as a solution to the frogs, two alligators from a pet shop. Lee also acquires a girlfriend, Elizabeth, who lives the good life in Big Sur for nine months of the year, supported by working as a prostitute in Los Angeles the rest of the time. An off-beat idyll now seems possible.

Then Johnston Wade, owner of a San Jose insurance business, arrives. He is on the run from the pressures of consumerist culture in general and from the predatory materialism of his family in particular. Wade has $100,000 in a briefcase, two bottles of Jim Beam whiskey, some cheese and a pomegranate. He soon proves to be disturbed and disruptive, offering money to Elizabeth and Elaine to sleep with him, mechanically repeating details of his life "as if he were a prisoner of war, giving his name, rank and serial number" (CG 111) and heading off to start a brush fire. Lee puts him in a shed and ties him to a log. Meanwhile, Jesse is beginning to feel ambivalent about Lee, whom he previously seemed to admire for his ability to wish away anxieties. Italicised vignettes of the civil war are inserted into the text and in these Lee's great-grandfather becomes a scared private running from the fight rather than the imagined heroic general that Jesse promised to believe in. Jesse is losing faith in Lee Mellon and his narratives. Elaine seems to offer Jesse an alternative and much more tangible sense of fulfilment. But Jesse finds this promised land of love as unsatisfying as the promised land of Big Sur. In the penultimate scene, Elaine is using various ploys to arouse him sexually and Jesse responds to each of them by failing to get an erection (CG 138–140). It is an actual and symbolic moment of impotence. After this comes the novel's most flamboyant metafictional gesture – an endless succession of endings.

Most critics who reviewed *Confederate General* for newspapers and magazines assumed it was a Beat novel, and therefore part of what many considered an unappealing and temporary phenomenon. *Playboy*'s anonymous reviewer, for instance, saw *Confederate General* as "a surrealist synopsis of everything that was worth missing in the now-fading beat literary scene" ("Books"). Ironically, it is a parody of that scene rather than a last hurrah, even though, initially, Lee seems to be the equivalent of Dean Moriarty in Kerouac's *On the*

Road. He is a restless outsider with criminal tendencies, an autodidact, and a roguishly engaging character (at least for the narrator). But Dean, through the eyes of his chronicler, retains a romantic aura, whereas Lee's quickly fades. Dean is presented as a charismatic folk hero, an icon for youngsters chafing at the restraints and hypocrisies of mainstream America. He is part Jesse James, part Rimbaud or Baudelaire, part hustling hipster, and part visionary mystic. Nothing in Jesse's narration suggests that level of admiration and nothing in Lee's actions and words suggest that it would be appropriate. Later, a more sceptical Jesse can say of him: "Lee Mellon fell apart at the edges like tobacco crumbling" (CG 93). Lee is reprising Dean's counter-cultural hero role as farce. His rebellion against the establishment consists of cheating the gas company so ineptly that the gas he steals produces a dangerously unmanageable six-foot flame (CG 34). Otherwise, his outlaw credentials consist of a sneak attack on a man who gives him a lift (CG 12) and a $6.72 raid on two boys. Whereas Dean, according to *On the Road*, is among those who are "mad to be saved" (5), Lee is no seeker of spiritual insights. His quest seems to consist of getting by as comfortably as he can while refusing to work, in trusting on self-delusion to make life seem satisfactory, in hoping to get drunk and laid along the way with, perhaps, some drugs thrown in from time to time. All of which seems to position Lee as a sharp contrast to Dean. I would argue, though, that Lee is not the antithesis of Kerouac's hero but simply a less deceived way of viewing him. In *On the Road*, the mantra of self-expression and spontaneity often looks every bit as self-centred as the capitalist values that the Beats deplored. *Confederate General* draws attention to this by offering a Dean whose failings are exposed through comic exaggeration rather than excused or not even recognised. In doing so, it presents a satire of Beat pretentions and romanticism.

Confederate General also has strong narrative links to two other Kerouac novels, *The Dharma Bums* and *Big Sur*. In the first, Ray Smith, a fictionalised Kerouac, seeks spiritual refreshment as a lone fire watcher in a mountain look-out. In the second, a deeply disturbed Duluoz/Kerouac stays at a shack in Big Sur to try to regain some peace of mind. He fails, as does Jesse, but whereas in *The Dharma*

Bums and *Big Sur* we are expected to take the quest for healing through nature seriously, in *Confederate General* not even Jesse seems to care about it. His narration ends with a metaphorical shrug of the shoulders as he offers us virtually any ending we might choose. Again, Beat romanticism is revisited as farce.

Of course, the notion of escape through pastoral idyll is not confined to Beat literature but is one of America's most enduring literary themes, and can be found in works as various as Thoreau's *Walden*, Twain's *Adventures of Huckleberry Finn* and Hemingway's *The Sun Also Rises* and "Big Two-Hearted River". Tony Tanner associates this genre with a tendency to see with the "wondering eye" of a child (*Reign* 7). For Leslie A. Fiedler, though, this "retreat to nature and childhood" is disturbing rather than innocent, childish rather than child-like (*Love and Death* xxi). It is escape from one's responsibilities and also reflects what Fiedler sees as a characteristic failing among American writers: an inability to deal honestly and convincingly in their fiction with adult heterosexual relationships. Instead, their male heroes head for the hills, often bonding with another male, and hide from the problems of adulthood and civilisation.

Like many a grand narrative, Fiedler's thesis can be attacked for overstating its case. Nevertheless, his comments are an interesting prism through which to view *Confederate General.* Male bonding is a central motif and, in one way and another, Wade, Lee and Jesse are all in flight from women as well as urban life. Also, a reasonable case can be made for judging their behaviour as childishly irresponsible. Lee is a liar, a cheat and a thief and refuses to accept responsibility when he makes a sixteen-year-old girl pregnant (CG 36); Jesse aids and abets him in much of this; Wade has family and corporate responsibilities from which he flees. Yet however one judges the behaviour of the characters, what is clear is that they are performing not merely a Beat parody but one in which a broad swathe of pastoral-romantic literature is satirised. In *Confederate General*, nature heals no wounds. In moving from the city to a shack at Big Sur, Jesse and Lee have merely exchanged one kind of slum for another. Jesse feels worse than ever and Lee simply carries on imagining his existence as he did in San Francisco.

Lee is central to the parodic enterprise, enabling the novel to satirise not only pastoral romantics but also a range of American beliefs/mythologies, including the pioneering spirit and the can-do mentality. He is an authentic American hero in that he overcomes all obstacles; but he triumphs only by imagining victory and is comically short of any heroic qualities. He sees himself as a proud rebel, descendent of a hero of the rebel South, but is a parody of principled non-conformity: as Jesse comments, Lee is "a Confederate general in ruins" (CG 9). His secession from society is not on any point of principle and he is perfectly happy to enjoy consumerism's prizes, as long as he can steal or scrounge them. As for pioneering self-reliance, Lee's trip into the wilds proves him to be a hunter who cannot put enough meat on the table before his inadequate supply of bullets runs out, a cook whose staple food is inedible, and a homesteader whose shelter is dangerously ramshackle. As the hapless Lee slowly rises from the floor, after passing out following a drinking session, Jesse's ironic summation of his friend is this: "The end product of American spirit, pride, and the old know-how" (CG 81). Lee Mellon also gives us a scrounger's version of the American Dream: it involves finding discarded cigarette butts for recycling into home-rolls. In pursuit of this dream, like the early white explorers of the American West, Lee sets out on expeditions of discovery.

> Sometimes he would find a gathering of cigarette butts like a ring of mushrooms in an enchanted forest, but sometimes he would have to walk a mile for a cigarette butt. Then he would flash a six-toothed wonder when he finally found one. In other lands it might be called a smile.
>
> Sometimes after he had walked a half a mile or so and hadn't found a cigarette butt, he would get very depressed and have a fantasy that he would never find another cigarette butt, that he would walk all the way to Seattle without finding one on the highway, and he would turn east and walk all the way to New York, looking carefully month after month along the highway for a cigarette butt without ever finding one. Not a damn one, and the end of an American Dream. (CG 92)

Yet Lee achieves the contentment that the American Dream and its associated mythologies are supposed to deliver, a steady state of satisfaction lacking in Johnston Wade, the entrepreneur who seems to "have it all". Lee's version of being a self-made man is to refashion himself through delusion. His experience and that of Wade suggest that the fruits of the American Dream are illusory; the only way to enjoy them is by imagining that they have been gathered in.

Such themes emerge clearly enough within the text. However, problems arise with their interpretation, and that of the characters, because Brautigan applies parody not only to what occurs within the narrative and to genre, but to the very nature of narrative discourse. The multiple endings are the most obvious and significant example. The main narrative finishes with Jesse and Elaine's abortive love-making. Five different endings are then offered, some of which are in conflict and therefore leave us uncertain about how to interpret the narrative as a whole. In one, for instance, Wade seems to have abandoned his bohemian experiment for good; in another he returns and throws all his money into the sea. But the most profound problem of interpretation comes when the narrator then declares that the novel is having more and more endings, none of which is specified, until in the final line Jesse tells us that they are occurring at the speed of light: 186,000 of them every second. The range of possibilities is now as near infinite as we can grasp. Thus the focus moves from interpreting events and themes within the narrative to the nature of the narrative form itself and the conventions it employs.

This acute awareness of novelistic devices, and their theatrical exposure to the reader, places *Confederate General* in the same metafictional category as American novels of the time such as Kurt Vonnegut's *Slaughterhouse-Five,* John Barth's *The Sot-Weed Factor,* Thomas Pynchon's *The Crying of Lot 49,* Donald Barthelme's *Snow White,* and William H. Gass's *Willie Masters' Lonesome Wife.* It undermines its own narrative credibility by offering a plethora of possible endings, by blurring the line between fiction and conventional notions of historical reality and by offering two narratives from different eras – the American Civil War and contemporary California – and presenting them as a single strand. Marc Chénetier comments: "Brautigan fights to preserve the independence of the text from the constraints of conventional narrative discourse; the 'battle' the text offers us is not the one we have been led to expect." (26)

Of course, before the ending, conventional themes, characters and narrative sequences are undeniably present, and it is certainly legitimate to discuss them, as I have done. But it is a concern with the way language and its narrative structures operate that is most striking. This foregrounding of language is a further instance of the poetic sensibility of Brautigan. We see it in the book's celebration of metaphoric diction, which was so much a part of *Revenge* and *The Pill*. This is found mostly in the early pages, where unexpected comparisons and images crowd the text. The Big Sur Indians "reported like autumn" to the Confederate Army (CG 9); a cargo ship leaving San Francisco is imagined to be "carrying the hides of 163 cable cars" (CG 15); seagulls are "passing almost like drums to the sky" (CG 15); an opening car window "drifted effortlessly down like the neck of a transparent swan"(CG 55). By turns, the images are amusing, wistful or simply baffling. In the latter case, as with the comparison of seagulls and drums, Brautigan is employing the kind of self-subverting metaphor that we find in his poetry and in some of the short stories.

Such elements are a lively disruption of the text, just as Lee Mellon's attitudes and escapades are themselves a lively and disruptive presence. Hence, the texture of the language is mimicking a phenomenon within the narrative. It simulates the disruptive, freebooting exploits of Lee, as perceived by Jesse. As the component parts of metaphors and similes strain or fail to connect, the text's language is joining the characters in seeking escape from conventional existence – in this case from the necessity of conforming to accepted ways of constructing narrative meaning. As the narrative focus moves more towards Jesse, and as Jesse's attitude to Lee becomes ambivalent, so the flow of metaphors eases and the text loses much of it playfulness and swagger. The metaphors and surreal images that remain tend to be melancholy. Soon Jesse is scoffing at an extravagant simile in his own narrative. Lee says that the waves at Big Sur " 'crack like eggs against the Grand Grill of North America'." He asks Jesse if he likes that comparison. Jesse responds: "'Ah, fuck it'" (CG 135). The text is becoming self-reflexive just as Jesse becomes more introspective. Two pages later, Jesse begins a whimsical simile of his own about the waves but it flounders and he cannot be bothered to rescue it:

> Elaine stared at the waves that were breaking like ice cube trays out of a monk's tooth or something like that. Who knows? I don't know. (CG 137)

The language is breaking up and soon the narrative structure falls apart as the multiple endings arrive. The narrative style and structure have faithfully mimicked narrative content and, more particularly, the consciousness of the narrator as presented in the narrative. Once more we are directed to the way that language is being used rather than to what it might formally signify.

Brautigan also stresses again and again the status of *Confederate General* as one text in a world of texts. Rather than fruitlessly rebelling against its dependence on what has already been written, *Confederate General* makes the debt apparent through a theatrically heightened level of allusion. Some 40 writers or texts are named. The authors range from Nietzsche, Schopenhauer and Kant to Dylan Thomas, Mark Twain, Henry Miller, John Donne, Jack London and Sappho. The named texts include Steinbeck's *In Dubious Battle*, "Ecclesiastes", Isaac Babel's "Red Cavalry", Patchen's *The Journal of Albion Moonlight* and William Carlos Williams's *Journey to Love*. Quotations from real and imagined texts take up some ten pages, most notably the 8½ pages of letters between Lee and Jesse (CG 41–49) and a long quotation from Ezra J. Warner's *Generals in Gray* (CG 20–21), the reference work in which Lee Mellon's civil war ancestor is vainly sought. The "Ecclesiastes" reference is particularly interesting because it introduces a double layer of allusion. In the chapter entitled "The Rivets in Ecclesiastes" (61–63), Jesse tells us:

> I was, of course, reading Ecclesiastes at night in a very old Bible that had heavy pages. At first I read it over and over again every night, and then I read it once every night, and then I began reading just a few verses every night, and now I was just looking at the punctuation marks.
>
> Actually I was counting them, a chapter every night. I was

putting the number of punctuation marks down in a notebook, in neat columns. I called the notebook "The Punctuation Marks in Ecclesiastes." I thought it was a nice title. I was doing it as a kind of study in engineering.

Certainly before they build a ship they know how many rivets it takes to hold the ship together and the various sizes of the rivets. I was curious about the number of rivets and the sizes of those rivets in Ecclesiastes, a dark and beautiful ship sailing on our waters. (CG 61–62)

Malley notes (107–108) how, apart from the obvious Biblical allusion, the incident echoes a text mentioned earlier: Hemingway's "Big Two-Hearted River". In this, the tale's protagonist, Nick, immerses himself in detailed tasks, minutely described, to retain or to help restore the precarious balance of his mind. This further level of allusion deepens the resonance of the passage. Malley also identifies a variety of other occasions where style or content point to other texts or writers. These include the italicised civil war passages towards the book's end, which recall the italicised vignettes of Hemingway's *In Our Time* and passages in Stephen Crane's *The Red Badge of Courage* (Malley 101). Malley also notes that Lee's illegal gas-tapping is a parodic reprise of the illegal electricity-tapping by the hero of Ralph Ellison's *Invisible Man* (98). More broadly, one can point to *Confederate General*'s central narrative premise, that of escape to Big Sur, as drawing directly on Kerouac's *Big Sur*, just as the character of Lee Mellon draws directly on that of *On the Road*'s Dean Moriarty. To this thicket of intertextuality we can also add the fact that the targets of *Confederate General*'s playful parodies are frequently literary: Beat literature, pastoral-escape literature in general and, most radically, the conventions of narrative discourse. Whatever else it may be, *Confederate General* is a book about books, and one constructed to a significant extent out of fragments real or imagined from the textual world to which it belongs.

Chapter Four: Language as mindscape

In Watermelon Sugar

Confederate General offers subversions of perceived reality, but *In Watermelon Sugar* proposes a wholly different reality. The action is set in a place whose main construction material is watermelon sugar, whose sun shines in different colours and whose ancestors may or may not have been tigers. iDEATH is the community's "downtown" or residence – which of the two is uncertain but, in any case, it is constantly shape-shifting, so indeterminacy is its identity. Apart from central iDEATH's perpetual flux, everything in the wider iDEATH community seems to operate in predictable and desired patterns, including the habits and conversations of the citizens; even the sun's changes of colour occur predictably. More importantly, iDEATH is not only an imagined reality but a concept, a way of living which attempts to suppress aspects of human nature such as passion, aggression, acquisitiveness, introspection and even simple curiosity about the nature of one's existence. To imagine, to be inquisitive or to desire can lead to dissatisfaction. Only a positive, directed use of the imagination is encouraged – one which seems to aim at the kind of contentment conjured into existence by *Confederate General*'s Lee Mellon. The suppression is voluntary, it seems, and is symbolised by the lower-case "i" of iDEATH; traditional notions of self-hood, represented by the capital "I", are now dead. The objective appears to be a life involving as little pain, guilt, grief or fear as possible. The rustic, low-tech iDEATH community can be read as a projection of a possible future, perhaps one following a natural or man-made catastrophe. Or, considering phenomena such as the colour-changing sun, it could be an imagined planet or parallel universe. The most fruitful approach, I think, is to consider iDEATH as a symbolic mindscape.

The book has a first-person narrator who says that he has no "regular name" (WS 4); he asks us to call him "whatever is in your mind" (WS 4), recalling the instability of the author's own identity as Brautigan, then Porterfield, then Brautigan again. Two interwoven histories are provided: the narrator's and that of the iDEATH community. The focus in the former is the break-up of one romance and the establishment of another. The story of the community begins during a time in the narrator's childhood when iDEATH is being preyed upon by tigers. As one might expect in a Brautigan world, these are not tigers as we know them: they talk the same language as the community they devour, are capable of great affability, tell good stories and have beautiful singing voices. They symbolise the dangerous animal appetites of humanity, but also its capacity for creativity and, perhaps, passionate engagement. One day, the tigers attack the narrator's parents in front of him and eat them. Afterwards, the narrator is told by the community's leading figure, Charley, that the tigers must be exterminated, just as the community tries to exterminate characteristics that the tigers represent. They are hunted down and the last of the species ceremonially burned. At the point of cremation, a trout hatchery is built, replacing symbols of death with those of regeneration.

But the threat of the tigers is not the only one to be faced: there is also a potential internal challenge caused by dissidents. The first of these nay-sayers is Charley's brother, the aptly named inBOIL, who finds himself increasingly at odds with the passionless, unquestioning attitudes of iDEATH. He leaves to build his own shack at the edge of a *terra incognita*, bordering iDEATH's hinterland, which is known as the Forgotten Works. This is a seemingly unpopulated wasteland, huge and shunned by the majority of the community. It is the ruins of a previous civilisation, it seems. Unlike iDEATH, it produced many books, which the citizens of iDEATH re-cycle as fuel for their fires. From time to time, inBOIL is joined by other malcontents. According to the admittedly-biased narrator, inBOIL and his followers spend much of their time drunk on whiskey made with materials from the Forgotten Works, confirming that place as symbolic of damaging and rejected cultural habits.

As the action moves to the recent past, the narrator escorts his girlfriend, Margaret, on a visit to the Forgotten Works and meets inBOIL. Unlike Margaret, the narrator is hostile to inBOIL and indifferent to the unspecified objects which Margaret wants to collect from the Works. Her non-conformist attitudes begin to disappoint/ puzzle/anger him and soon he is turning his attention to Pauline, a woman with much more conventional views and interests. Meanwhile there is speculation in iDEATH about Margaret's relationship with inBOIL's faction, who are feared as potential insurgents. Indeed, they do "invade" iDEATH, although not to destroy it but to destroy themselves. They commit mass suicide at the trout hatchery, a place with such a central, shrine-like role in iDEATH. They cut off their thumbs, noses, ears and fingers until they bleed to death. inBOIL cries out that this self-destruction, achieved by severing body parts needed for three of the senses, is the true meaning of iDEATH, whose citizens have desensitised their lives. The community feels no grief or horror. Charley's immediate comment after the carnage is, "'Well, that's that'" (WS 96). The dead are not given iDEATH's normal ritual burial in glass coffins in a stream. Instead they are taken to be cremated in their shacks, echoing the fate of the tigers. The trip to the shacks becomes an "almost festive" parade (WS 99), with children picking flowers along the way, so that the procession is "a kind of vase filled with roses and daffodils and poppies and bluebells" (WS 99). An identification with 1960s' "flower children" is irresistible, suggesting that this might be an addition to the original text of 1964, which would have pre-dated the hippies. As the bodies are about to be burned, Margaret emerges from the Forgotten Works, is told what has happened, and is "very shocked, dazed" (WS 101). She grasps the narrator's hand but he offers no comfort. Soon, he becomes Pauline's lover, although he makes no formal break with Margaret. Instead he avoids her attempts to contact him and she is left to draw the conclusion that she has been rejected.

We learn about the repetitive routines of daily life in the community, the ritualisation of the details in which the citizens immerse themselves, as if undergoing some form of occupational therapy. Food, trivial gossip and simple routines of work are the focus of attention; intellectual and literary activities are absent. No excess of emotion, whether of joy or sorrow, is felt, or at least expressed. The narrator speaks of his relationship with Pauline in terms no more enthusiastic than those used to describe the folksy communal meals that are the earnest subject of so much conversation. Nevertheless, the apparently calm surface of this existence has undercurrents of unease. For instance, Pauline is an insomniac until her affair with the narrator and cannot help feeling some guilt about replacing Margaret. The narrator also suffers from insomnia, unrelieved by the affair, and goes for long night walks. Furthermore, he has a suspect preference for Thursdays, which are black and soundless. Still, both characters manage to function within community norms. The one person who cannot do so, because she cannot master her emotions, is Margaret. Already an outsider in some of her interests, and under suspicion because of her lack of hostility to inBOIL, she now has to cope with silent rejection by her lover. She hangs herself from an apple tree. Pauline is distressed and seems to feel some responsibility. She recovers, however, calmed rather than repelled by the narrator's neutral response to the jilted Margaret's suicide. He tells Pauline: " 'It was nobody's fault. Just one of those things'" (WS 122). Margaret's brother is saddened by her death, but quickly accepts it as being "for the best" and agrees with the narrator that no-one is to blame (WS 118). Indeed, Margaret's death is attended by symbols of renewal: on the morning that she dies a child is born and after her burial the citizens gather at the trout hatchery, symbol of regeneration, for a traditional post-funeral dance. The book ends with musicians poised to play and a new day soon to dawn. Another dance is waiting to begin, a miniaturised version of the slow, formal dance that is the community's mode of being.

Tony Tanner sees iDEATH as "a happy commune" whose members are "well rid of the death-obsessed, trash-minded defectors" ("The Dream"). This is probably the majority critical view. Malley writes of "idyllic iDEATH" (116); Lew Welch, a San Francisco-based writer, who knew Brautigan, describes iDEATH as "a world of love and peace and simple reward". Yet indifference to the suffering of others is not the mark of a collective ethic; rather it denotes a particularly ruthless form of individualism. Also, although the narrator describes iDEATH as a "gentle place", he is involved in the events that he describes and must earn our trust like any other participant-narrator. When, therefore, he calmly recounts horrors and tragedies in a tone which suggests that nothing much has occurred, and records his own responses as being as disengaged as the narrative voice, we must wonder if his notion of a "gentle place" is one that we should accept. This is the narrator's description of his parents being killed and eaten, and of his response to it at the time:

> One of the tigers started eating my mother. He bit her arm off and started chewing on it. "What kind of story would you like to hear? I know a good story about a rabbit."
> "I don't want to hear a story," I said.
> "OK," the tiger said, and he took a bite out of my father. I sat there for a long time with the spoon in my hand, and then I put it down.
> "Those were my folks," I said, finally. (WS 33–34)

The tigers agree to answer some maths questions for the boy who then goes outside while the tigers finish eating. About an hour later the tigers emerge to remark on the fineness of the day and to offer an apology, which the child accepts:

> "All right," I said. "And thanks for helping me with my arithmetic."
> "Think nothing of it."
> The tigers left. (WS 35)

One way of acknowledging iDEATH's lack of compassion is to propose that it is a dystopian vision rather than a utopia, or that the tranquillity it might produce comes at too high an ethical price. Neil Schmitz, for one, argues that people of iDEATH have achieved a seemingly idyllic existence only through "a disfiguring of their humanity"; Jay Boyer stresses the essential selfishness of iDEATH's inhabitants (30); Robert Adams describes *Watermelon* as "a fable, but also a nightmare, of innocence" (24). Patricia Hernlund, one of the most outspoken opponents of the iDEATH-as-Eden critics, says of Brautigan's book: "It is not a description of 'the students' way of life' or a lyric description of a successful counterculture. Brautigan judges his utopian commune and finds it wanting...." (17)

However, if Brautigan disapproves of iDEATH, as Hernlund maintains, where is his disapproval to be found? James Dishon McDermott makes an important point when he writes of Brautigan's self-effacement in *Watermelon* (64–65). The narration is handed to a character who is himself an extreme example of self-effacement, a person whose very name is contingent upon what we call him, someone trying to erase many of the instincts which we associate with self-hood. McDermott identifies him as being unidentifiable, a "blank self" (66). He does express a point of view, of course, one which endorses iDEATH's principles; but, as I have suggested, there is good reason not to privilege his opinions, and certainly no reason to equate them with the author's. Neither does the text privilege any of the alternative voices, such as inBOIL's or Margaret's. What we are left with, therefore, is not a text with a point of view but a neutral text in which a montage of views is presented. inBOIL's view is the one most opposed to the narrator's. Margaret, on the other hand, seems broadly in accord with iDEATH's norms when we first meet her, except for her sense of curiosity. But she has both passion and compassion, two qualities suppressed in the iDEATH mode of being and, like inBOIL, she is destroyed by her vulnerability. Fred, a manager at iDEATH's watermelon factory, and Pauline, have been unable to completely desensitise themselves but are sufficiently capable of controlling their emotions to avoid the extreme vulnerability of inBOIL and Margaret. Charley is capable of feelings, but suppresses them even more rigorously. On the surface, the narrator seems to be the most successful at self-suppression, but chronic insomnia and a liking for the black sun are surely symptoms of the psychiatric strain that this suppression causes him.

Each of these characters is described in terms of their response to iDEATH's code of behaviour and modes of thought. In the process, *Watermelon* becomes a case study of how we might cope with the knowledge and pain of our mortality without the consolation of religion – a theme also found in *Confederate General*. The conclusion appears to be this: if we can suppress our tigerish appetites, and much else besides, then we can soothe the pains of existence. In effect, then, iDEATH aspires to be a community of Lee Mellons; as Tony Tanner suggests ("The Dream"), its main building material, the sweetly insubstantial watermelon sugar, is intended to represent that sweetly intangible transformer, the human imagination. However, in return for our peace of mind we must accept a numbing of the intellectual, creative, passionate and compassionate aspects of our nature. The text presents us with no choice of its own. It offers a mindscape, and it can just as well be considered that of a single consciousness as it can be that of a multiplicity of them. Such a reading chimes with post-modern ideas of the mind as a plurality of possible "selves". Here, then, is a mind struggling towards the perfection of iDEATH consciousness, but deeply conflicted about the price to be paid. It knows, too, that the physical representation of that perfected consciousness is in a permanent state of flux; arrival may seem imminent, but the destination has always moved on.

A sense of what achieving the ideal might feel like is provided by the trance-like quality of the language. As in *Confederate General*, the texture of the language simulates a consciousness expressed within the narrative. The tone is set in the first sentence: "In watermelon sugar the deeds were done and done again as my life is done in watermelon sugar." (WS 1) An underlying iambic metre gives a subtle flow to the sentence, complemented by the double repetition of "done", which has a sonorous bell-tolling effect, and by the five-times-repeated consonant "d"; the closure of the sentence with the same phrase with which it began adds a ceremonial, incantatory air, heightened by the formality of expression produced by the syntactical inversion which makes "In watermelon sugar" the opening phrase. A gently rhythmic, otherworldly and ritualistic tone is established; a pattern of repetition and circularity emerges. Already in this first sentence, a simulacrum of iDEATH consciousness and community life is being formed. Three pages later, in the chapter called "My Name", a much more extended example occurs, with "That is my name." repeated at set intervals like a chant or a song's refrain, and each intervening verse beginning alternately with "Or" or "Perhaps".

If you are thinking about something that happened a long time ago: Somebody asked you a question and you did not know the answer.

That is my name.

Perhaps it was raining very hard.

That is my name.

Or somebody wanted you to do something. You did it. Then they told you what you did was wrong – "Sorry for the mistake," – and you had to do something else.

That is my name.

Perhaps it was a game that you played when you were a child or something that came idly into your mind when you were old and sitting in a chair near the window.

That is my name.

Or you walked someplace. There were flowers all around.

That is my name.

Perhaps you stared into a river. There was somebody near you who loved you. They were about to touch you. You could feel this before it happened. Then it happened.

That is my name.

Or you heard someone calling from a great distance. Their voice was almost an echo.

That is my name.

Perhaps you were lying in bed, almost ready to go to sleep and you laughed at something, a joke unto yourself, a good way to end the day.

That is my name.

Or you were eating something good and for a second forgot what you were eating, but still went on, knowing it was good.

That is my name.

Perhaps it was around midnight and the fire tolled like a bell inside the stove.

That is my name.

Or you felt bad when she said that thing to you. She could have told it to someone else: somebody who was more familiar with her problems.

That is my name.

Perhaps the trout swam in the pool but the river was only eight inches wide and the moon shone on iDEATH and the watermelon

fields glowed out of proportion, dark and the moon seemed to
rise from every plant.
  That is my name. (WS 4–5)

The simple formality of the structure is echoed in the simple formality of the language. There are no colloquial contractions and the
rhythm and diction have a Biblical feel. These give the text a slightly
archaic, mythic, ceremonial tone, increased by the unexpected use
of the word "unto". Towards the end, the sense of otherworldliness
intensifies. First Brautigan introduces one of his strikingly unexpected similes: a fire that tolls like a bell. Next comes a situation
whose meaning is too obscure to guess at: a woman saying something unpalatable and, to us, unknowable. In the final, most lyrically
intense section, the moon seems to be rising from every watermelon
plant and trout are swimming in eight-inch streams.

  There are clear parallels between the character of *Watermelon*'s
language and the state of consciousness sought in the psychedelic
multi-media events of the 1960s which are so much associated with
San Francisco, and memorably recorded in Wolfe's *The Electric
Kool-Aid Acid Test*. Hypnotic, repetitive rock beats, surreal light
shows and LSD would combine to produce a hoped-for state of
disengaged bliss. The dream-like flow of *Watermelon*'s language is
the literary equivalent of "turning on", of being "far out". To that
extent, *Watermelon* is a psychedelic novel and iDEATH consciousness
the perfect high. The language's simulation of this consciousness
is helped by the disengaged tone of the narrator. He may speak
approvingly of his community, and disapprovingly of inBOIL and
Margaret, but the dominant tone is emotionally neutral, as when he
reports on his parents' death. Just as iDEATH consciousness requires
one to float serenely over the tragedies afflicting others, so the text
floats serenely over the tragic events it describes. It has a painless
neutrality of response that the characters, including the narrator,
never fully attain.

  Another important element in creating this textual iDEATH is the
allusiveness of the language. The most prominent allusions are linked
to Christian tradition and thus heighten the text's mythic quality. For
example, Malley connects the warning at the gates of the Forgotten

Works to that at the entrance to Dante's hell (123). Dante has, in part, "ABANDON EVERY HOPE, ALL YOU WHO ENTER." (Canto III, 89), which Brautigan revisits, more colloquially and prosaically, as: "THIS IS THE ENTRANCE TO THE FORGOTTEN WORKS / BE CAREFUL / YOU MIGHT GET LOST". For the iDEATH community, the Forgotten Works is a kind of hell on earth, a place where you most certainly could lose your way, literally and metaphorically, a place for "lost souls" such as inBOIL and Margaret. There are also a series of direct Biblical allusions, which Harvey Leavitt identifies, in the contrasting attitudes and behaviour of Margaret and the narrator. One of Margaret's vices, in the eyes of the community, is her curiosity, exhibited in her fascination with the Forgotten Works. She hangs herself from an apple tree – the tree of knowledge in Genesis – and thus is identified by Leavitt with the Biblical Eve. The narrator is identified with a new and improved Adam because, in this revised version of Eden, he rejects Eve's advances. This is presented literally in the narrative, but also metaphorically through another Biblical allusion. In the chapter titled "Apple Pie" (WS 108–109), the narrator refuses a waitress's offer of a slice from that pie.

In the structure of *Watermelon,* we find once more a stress on ritualised repetition. For instance, each of the three major time frames covered in the novel has a death or deaths at its core. The relatively remote past has the deaths of the narrator's parents and the tigers, the recent past the suicide of inBOIL and his followers, and the present the suicide of Margaret. At key moments associated with death, a trout appears to the narrator in ways that suggest a symbolic significance. This happens three times (WS 34, 52–53, 114), and we find that many other things come in threes: three main time frames, three sections to the novel, three days during which the action of the most recent time frame takes place, three central characters. If one wished to push the notion of religious allusion even further, one could see in this repeated theme of triads a reference to their religious significance: the holy trinity, Peter's three denials of Christ and the supposed resurrection of the crucified Christ on the third day.

Dreams are another recurring feature, including the entire central section of the book being told as a dream of the narrator. Similarly, the book's title, repeated in the first line of the novel, recurs again and again, as do phrases such as "it's for the best" or variations of "it suits us". Another repeated motif comes when the image of a moth balanced on an apple (WS 60) is later followed by the apple pie that is rejected by the narrator and finally by the apple tree from which Margaret hangs herself (another trinity of images). The balancing moth can be traced back to a comment by the narrator, who says of iDEATH that it has "a delicate balance" (WS 1). In turn, moths crop up again, hovering above some tombs (WS 26). Finally, there is the repetition and circularity provided by the book's self-reflexive structure. The narrator begins by saying that he will tell us the story of iDEATH and includes two pages (WS 8–9) of numbered notes outlining what will follow. Throughout the book, various citizens ask the narrator about the book he is writing – the book that we are reading and in which their queries are recorded/imagined. The novel ends with a comma followed by the words "I wrote". These return us to the promise of a narrative act that was made at the outset and signal that the act is complete. They also stress the artifice of the performance, shifting our final focus from the illusion generated by the text to an image of a writer constructing that illusion. To emphasise the point, Brautigan adds a note immediately after the formal ending telling us where and when the story was written. As in *Confederate General*, a theme or themes can be found, but just as important – arguably, more important – is a clear fascination with manipulating language and narrative structures.

Chapter Five: Escape from the tomb of words

The Abortion: An Historical Romance 1966

In *Watermelon* and *Confederate General*, it is the manner in which the narratives are told which expresses the texts' focus on language and literary structures; in *The Abortion*, the narrative itself is a symbolic expression of this focus as Brautigan constructs an allegory of escape from the perceived tyranny of texts.

The story is narrated by the custodian of a very Brautiganesque institution – a library which subverts all expectation by neither lending books nor admitting readers and by accepting only unpublished work. As with *Watermelon*, the narrator is unnamed, and in both novels this depersonalisation helps emphasise the character of the language rather than that of the narrator. The narrator has spent three years in sole occupation of his San Francisco library, never going outside its door. He says that the library's main purpose is to make its writers feel appreciated and "to gather pleasantly together the unwanted, the lyrical and haunted volumes of American writing'" (TA 72). Or, as his girlfriend, Vida, puts it: the place is a library for losers (TA 39). The titles of the books include *Growing Flowers by Candlelight in Hotel Rooms*, by a woman who devotes much of her life to doing just that, and *The Other Side of My Hand*, a book about masturbation by a sixteen-year-old boy. In an archly self-reflexive touch, there is also a book called *Moose*, by someone called Richard Brautigan: "The author was tall and blond and had a long yellow moustache that gave him an anachronistic appearance. He looked as if he would be more at home in another era" (TA 23). Some other books had previously been deposited by this man, alluding to the fact that novels by the non-fictional Brautigan suffered rejection from publishers for quite a while.

Vida arrives at the library with a book of her own, which is about her belief that she is living in the wrong body. That body is a perfectly executed example of the preferred mode of female beauty and men have died for it. One committed suicide because Vida did not want him, another crashed his car and killed himself while distracted by Vida as she walked nearby. She has come to see her body as a curse. The librarian comforts her, they make love, and she moves into the library with him. Not long after she becomes pregnant. The couple agree that they are not mature enough for parenthood and decide on an abortion, illegal at that place and time. The librarian contacts someone he feels will know a way to get the job done. This is Foster, a hell-raising custodian of the caves that hold the library's archives, a character with some of the qualities of Lee Mellon in *Confederate General*, just as the quiet librarian is somewhat reminiscent of *Confederate General*'s Jesse. Foster knows just the man for abortions: a Dr. Garcia in Tijuana, across the Mexican border from San Diego. Foster raises money for the operation and flights and agrees to man the library while the couple are away.

The abortion is successful, with no complications, but the passages that describe it, and two other abortions, are sufficiently arresting in their spareness and eye for significant detail to communicate the chilling nature of the experience. Vida recovers and the couple head back to San Francisco, where they find Foster on the steps of the library. He tells them that he and they have been evicted. A woman who brought a book to the library took exception to Foster's slovenly appearance, and to any librarian who would allow someone such as Foster to deputise for him. Consequently she has taken charge of the place and dumped the few belongings of Vida and the narrator on the steps. The librarian must now return to "the real world." With Vida and Foster, he moves into a house in Berkeley. Vida works part-time as a topless dancer to earn money to go back to college and the narrator becomes a counter-cultural hero to the students of UC Berkeley, much as Brautigan himself became a hero at campuses across America. His role at the college is merely to sit at a table on the campus and collect donations for the library's mysterious owners, The American Forever, Etc. Everyone, it seems, will live happily ever after.

The opening passage has the gently poetic flow of *Watermelon*:

> This is a beautiful library, timed perfectly, lush and American. The hour is midnight and the library is deep and carried like a dreaming child into the darkness of these pages....
>
> I have been sitting at this desk for hours, staring into the darkened shelves of books. I love their presence, the way they honour the wood they rest upon.
>
> I know it's going to rain.
>
> Clouds have been playing with the blue style of the sky all day long, moving their heavy black wardrobes in, but so far nothing rain has happened. (TA 11)

This passage sets the tone for the opening section. Like *Confederate General* and *Watermelon*, the prose style simulates an element of the narrative. In this case, as in the passage above, the language has a strangeness, and a kind of hushed, ritualised reverence that parallels the narrative's description of the library and the librarian's existence within it. The passage abounds with Brautiganisms, from the opening simile and final metaphor to the sudden non-sequitur of "I know it's going to rain"; then there is the curiously phrased "nothing rain has happened" and the unexplained notion of a library being "timed perfectly".

The rituals and the sanctuary-like status of the library, as well as the way that the language seems to reflect these, cause Boyer to suggest that what we might have here is a symbolic representation of *Watermelon*'s iDEATH (31). Malley, on the other hand, wonders if the library might not symbolise America itself, or at least aspects of it, and therefore its "timid, strange, insecure librarians are comic equivalents of American presidents" (67–68). He points out that the narrator believes himself to be the 35th or 36th librarian (TA 19). In 1966, the year in which the book is set, Lyndon Johnson was the 35th or 36th president of the United States, depending on whether Grover Cleveland's two non-consecutive terms are counted once or twice. Malley also notes that the library is said to have been in New York, then moved to St. Louis and finally to San Francisco, reflecting the movement west of the United States. The narrator also tells us that the library "has a lot of Dutch books somewhere." (TA 28), which suggests that it dates back to the early days of European settlement, when New York was New Amsterdam. The title of the library's shadowy owners, America Forever, Etc., also speaks of longevity and territorial inclusiveness. Malley says: "The library ... seems to be a kind of metaphor for the loneliness of American experience and for the need to communicate" (67). Alternatively, the library can be seen as a shelter from the degraded, consumerist culture around it. This appears to be the position of Jim Langlois, who argues that Brautigan "declares a war of gentle violence waged by the imagination on the emptiness of contemporary life." Equally, the library can be considered a place of death or exile: Foster compares it to a funeral parlour (TA 71) and Vida finds it " 'a creepy place' " (TA 39); also, Chénetier points out that the library's literal role is to be a morgue for "defunct writings" (32), a notion that I will develop later.

The trip to Mexico provides further speculation on the narrative's symbolic role. James M. Mellard stresses the journey as a mission of death, interpreting it, in Dante-esque terms, as a "journey to the underworld" (147). For William Bedford Clark, though, the trip is a rebirth for the librarian who, with Vida's help, is able to come to terms with life – although, ironically, via the pursuit of a death. Symbols of birth and rebirth accompany the journey: children playing outside the clinic (TA 131, 148) and Easter displays in the Tijuana branch of Woolworth's with "yellow chicks bursting happily out of huge eggs." (TA 125) Malley notes other similar symbols: an advertising sign in which a chicken holds a "gigantic egg" is noticed on the way to San Francisco Airport (TA 97); the colour green, symbolic of Spring, is frequently mentioned, including the Green Hotel, where the couple stop briefly in San Diego, and most ironically, the green-painted abortion clinic; finally, the very fact that the journey is undertaken in Spring is symbolic of rebirth (Malley 78) as, of course, is the Christian feast of Easter. Vida's name is itself symbolic, the Spanish word for life, which is what she brings to the librarian even as she condemns her foetus to death by travelling to Spanish-speaking Mexico. Malley sees the narrator as a "hero of our time" (89), a quiet, well-intentioned, caring man trying to do good in a bad world; his rise to campus hero is therefore well deserved.

Actually, the narrator's sudden heroic status is one of the narrative's least convincing elements. We are not told why the narrator becomes lionised and are given insufficient information to make any guesses. The librarian appears to have some "gentle hippie" values, but the Berkeley campus was remarkable for its assertive, radical activism at the time rather than for its championing of gentle hippies. One reading that accounts for such an inadequately explained conclusion comes from Charles Hackenberry, who finds elements of genre parody at work. At one level, the text is a psycho-drama, with the library as a dominant subconscious and escape from it the triumph of the ego, but at another it is a parody of romance literature, which returns us to the genre parody of *Confederate General*. In support of this one can point to the parodic nature of the quest which the hero and heroine undertake. For them, the Holy Grail is an abortion in Tijuana. When they return in triumph to their castle they find that they have been evicted, and at the tale's conclusion the noble knight is a charity collector whose princess is a topless dancer. To be acclaimed a hero in such circumstances is a suitably ironic ending.

Hackenberry's analysis has merit and, indeed, it is difficult to exclude any of the interpretations I have listed. For instance, in support of the notion that the library symbolises America we can argue that the number of US presidents being exactly the same as the number of librarians is hardly likely to be a coincidence, particularly as the narrator takes care to note the uncertainty about whether he is the 35th or 36th custodian. Nevertheless, the library's role as a metaphor for the US is never developed (just as Vida's foetus is never allowed to develop), and one could argue that America is what happens outside the library; the latter's role is to comfort America's unwanted who, in a further irony, arrive at its door as migrants from America rather than to it. We also have the paradox that the library is not only a place of comfort but also a place of incarceration, for both the books and their custodian. The librarian may be slow to acknowledge the limitations of his text-bound existence but, encouraged by Vida and Foster, he grabs his chance for a new life on the outside and clearly has no regrets. However, such seemingly contradictory signals are only paradoxical if we insist on singular meaning, a comfort that Brautigan often denies us. In typically playful mode, he may simply have created symbolic links as they occurred to him, with no intention of following them through in any sustained, coherent fashion.

Brautigan's obsession with language, and his simultaneous frustration with language's limitations, provide the source for my own reading of *The Abortion*'s symbolism, one that is intended to stand alongside those previously mentioned rather than to supplant them. Many of those readings note characteristics of the library, and of the narrator's isolation, without appearing to grasp that they could easily apply to any situation in which a man chooses solitude within a large, old building. But this is a particular kind of establishment. As Chénetier reminds us, it is a morgue for books, and therefore the narrator lives surrounded by literary corpses. Just as the exaggerated intertextuality of *Confederate General* locates it in a textual universe, so too is the librarian located in a universe of texts, albeit one of his own making. Chénetier (32) links the notion of the library as a morgue to Brautigan's description of a book store in *Trout Fishing* as "a parking lot for used graveyards" (TF 22). This, in turn, brings to mind Chénetier's view that Brautigan saw writing as a liberating experience but also as an act of murder, because what it produced were fixed, dead texts. So many of these dead already exist that any author can feel imprisoned by them, and unable to avoid simply adding to them, using the same words, phrases and themes. Surely the librarian's position symbolises this situation. He isolates himself inside dead texts, steadily adds to those texts with more of the same and knows nothing of a life outside them.

Brautigan's attitude to the themes that emerge in his books often seems ambivalent, and that ambivalence extends to the very means through which those themes are expressed: genres of fiction, narrative discourse generally and, finally, language itself. In *Revenge*, the narrator of "The World War 1 Los Angeles Aeroplane" is trying to find words of comfort for his wife after her father has died, only to conclude, resignedly: "Always at the end of the words somebody is dead" (RL 142). Language can be frustratingly limited in its ability to effect change but also, paradoxically, you can find yourself tyrannised by language, which is what happens when the "paper shadows" descend on the narrator of "Corporal" (RL 99–100). Towards the end of *Confederate General* the narrator becomes exasperated by one of the most characteristic traits of Brautigan's writing, the surreal or self-subverting metaphor, and throughout the book, and particularly with the arrival of the endless endings, the author shows frustration with basic narrative conventions. In *The Abortion*, as noted above, a Richard Brautigan brings one of his books to be interred in the library. The narrator tells us that he has previously brought three or four others. *The Abortion* is commonly counted as Brautigan's fourth novel, but an extremely short (600 words) so-called novel, *The God of the Martians*, was written in the mid-1950s, following the manner of Brautigan's juvenilia. It was never published. So there are either three or four predecessors of *The Abortion*, depending on whether you include *Martians*. At the time that Brautigan was writing *The Abortion*, only *Confederate General* had been published, and that first edition was a commercial flop. Therefore, apart from any general reservations that Brautigan might have had about the novel as a genre, his own experience of trying to get his novels published and read had not been a happy one. The narrator of *The Abortion* has this to say about the Richard Brautigan who brings his latest book to be buried:

> Every time he brought in a new book he looked a little older, a little more tired. He looked quite young when he brought in his first book. I can't remember the title of it, but it seems to me the book had something to do with America. (TA 23)

The narrator asks him what his latest book is about. " 'Just another book,' he said" (TA 23). The whole passage, excerpted above, is playful in its self-reflexiveness and yet mournful. Just another book. Just another unwanted dead body to be added to the pile. Towards the end of the Mexican trip in *The Abortion*, the narrator follows the lead of *Confederate General*'s narrator by scoffing at one of Brautigan's literary trademarks. In *Confederate General* it is his use of metaphor; in *The Abortion* it is the attention paid to trivia. The librarian has been describing some events in Woolworth's Tijuana store and then, in minute detail, he explains the exact location of the store telephone that he uses, and follows it with this: "What a bunch of junk to remember, but that's what I remember and look forward to the time I forget it" (TA 125). This can be seen as an understandable desire to erase memories of a traumatic journey, but the narrator is writing after the successful completion of the trip. A more persuasive explanation, I think, is a desire on the part of the narrative's author to be free of the compulsion to record such details in a medium about which he feels ambivalent, seeking publishers who do not want to print his novels and a public who, on the one opportunity they have been given, seem not to want to read them. Vida/Life intervenes to provide the author with an escape by proxy from the textual into the extra-textual.

Brautigan's art frequently defies representational norms and, following the logic of that, in *The Abortion* it is an alternative to life rather than an imitation of it. Life is calling and the call cannot be answered without abandoning art. Symbolically, Brautigan makes his escape through that of the narrator but, paradoxically, that symbolic escape occurs through artistic performance, through a text recommending the abandonment of text. The escape is further symbolised by abandoning the exaggerated intertextuality which characterises *Trout Fishing* and *Confederate General*. As long as the action takes place inside the library, the narrative is literally located within other texts and is also, to a considerable extent, composed of them, because most of this early section concerns the reception, naming and description of books brought to the library, and the naming and description of their authors. Once the library is left behind, however, so is self-conscious intertextuality. Malley (73) detects an indirect allusion to Hemingway's "Hills Like White Elephants" (*First Forty-Nine* 262–266) in Brautigan's description of an abortion-bound American couple (TA 118–119, 121) but except for some references to *Playboy* magazine (TA 99,105,159), no text or author is mentioned.

The group of chapters covering the abortion itself offers another example of symbolic desertion of the textual universe. The section, Book Five, is entitled "My Three Abortions" (TA 129–148), referring to Vida's and two others carried out while she is in the clinic. Chénetier suggests a symbolic link between the three abortions and Brautigan's three previous San Francisco novels (55). Taken in isolation, this might seem an interpretation that is a mite too ingenious for its own good, but when considered as part of the pattern of symbolic meaning which I have argued for, the reading seems very plausible. As Chénetier notes, the Book Five title, with its possessive "My" rather than "The", strengthens the link to Brautigan's novels. Therefore it seems reasonable to equate the killing of the unwanted foetuses with the symbolic, ritualised destruction of Brautigan's unwanted novels. Two of those books, *Trout Fishing* and *Watermelon*, were themselves unborn in the sense that they had found no publisher, and *Confederate General* had been so little read that it, too, could be said to be unborn in terms of public consciousness. The narrator makes much of the ritual quality of the abortion process:

> The boy came into the room carrying the bucket and he went into the toilet and flushed the foetus and the abortion leftovers down the toilet.
> Just after the toilet flushed, I heard the flash of the instruments being sterilized by fire.
> It was the ancient ritual of fire and water all over again to be all over again and again in Mexico today. (TA 143)

It is a ritualised destruction of life, but also a ritualised destruction of the author's strongest connection to the textual universe he has inhabited – although, once more, this stylised renunciation of text is constructed through the medium of text. Once he is symbolically freed from his own works, and those of all the other writers symbolised by the library, Brautigan is able to imagine a happy, fulfilling life among the students of Berkeley. Beyond words, through purifying rituals of fire and water, he reaches rebirth as a campus hero.

As I have said, this happy ending in Berkeley has an unsatisfactory, throwaway feel to it. But if one is symbolically renouncing fictional narratives, and parodying the romance genre, then a flippant, unconvincing final scene is appropriate. Equally, if Brautigan is tired of the games that fiction plays, it may be the only ending that he can be bothered to provide. Certainly an air of carelessness pervades sections of the book, a lack of rigour that allows the tedious, the banal, the sentimental and the coyly whimsical to slip through. Such flaws mar some of his poems and short stories but are absent from *Watermelon*, and mostly absent from *Confederate General*. These books have a hard, undeceived edge to them that *The Abortion* lacks. One reason may be the hippie influence which undermines some of *The Pill*'s poems. Also, by the time *The Abortion* was being written, Brautigan's rigorous mentor/editor, Jack Spicer, was dead. It is impossible to believe that Spicer would not have put a pencil through the following passage from *The Abortion*, one describing part of the return flight to San Francisco:

> I pushed my face against the window and looked very hard and saw a star and I made a wish but I won't tell. Why should I? Purchase a cocktail from pretty Miss Zero and find your own star. *There's one for everyone in the evening sky* [my italics]. (TA 163)

Spicer might also have told Brautigan that anecdotes about men swooning helplessly at the sight of Vida can be amusing to start with but soon become exasperating when, at every small step of the narrative, we have accounts of new swoonings.

Nevertheless, the opening section in the library is as hauntingly effective as *Watermelon* and some of the defamiliarising, poet-as-stranger descriptions are well rendered. On the drive to San Francisco Airport, for instance, the narrator documents details of the scene that a jaded eye might never notice – a woman pushing a shopping trolley, an advertising hoarding, a man cleaning windows – and sums up his experience neatly enough: "I had forgotten how the streets in San Francisco go to get to the freeway. Actually, I had forgotten how San Francisco went" (TA 95). Also, when Brautigan drops into Hemingway mode for the chapters set in the clinic, the prose suddenly becomes lean, tense and graphic:

> There was a door that opened directly into an operating room. A teenage girl was in the room cleaning up and a young boy, another teenager, was helping her.
>
> A big blue flash of fire jumped across a tray full of surgical instruments. The boy was sterilizing the instruments with fire. It startled Vida and me. There was a table in the operating room

that had metal things to hold your legs and there were leather straps that went with them.

"No pain," the doctor said to Vida and then to me. "No pain and clean, all clean, no pain. Don't worry. No pain and clean. Nothing left. I'm a doctor," he said. (TA 133)

Such quality is rare outside the library, however, which is extremely frustrating because *The Abortion* abounds with imaginative notions. First there is the irresistible proposition of a library that admits no borrowers or readers and accepts only unpublished work. Then there is the figure of its solemn, solitary custodian who never leaves the building. Gradually a collage of symbols emerges, creating a variety of metaphorical perspectives from which to view the narrative, and frequently employing an appealing duality, as in Vida/Life bringing both death and rebirth. More generally – and most admirably – there is the ambitious allegorical structure that presents a writer fleeing from the frustrations of his textual universe, ritually renouncing his works and arriving in extra-textual bliss, courtesy of yet another text.

Chapter Six: Beyond metafiction

Trout Fishing in America

Trout Fishing in America is Brautigan's most innovative extended fiction. It is also one of the most significant books to emerge from the clutch of American challenges to conventional fiction mounted in the 1950s and 1960s. Some of these works, by Barth, Barthelme, Gass, Vonnegut and Pynchon, have been mentioned as a context within which to consider *Confederate General*. Typically, they show a metafictional concern with exposing the conventions of narrative discourse and emphasising its artificiality. Metafictional elements can also be found in *Watermelon Sugar* and *The Abortion*. In *Trout Fishing*, however, Brautigan goes beyond metafiction; the book certainly recycles some conventions from an ironic or playful perspective, but the main ones are simply ignored. Jonathan Culler points to theme, plot and character as the principal conventions, or what he calls "domains or sub-systems", of the novel (*Structuralist* 192), although not all need be present. Through these, the novel's referential data is organised and given significance to help us enter a "mimetic contract" with the text. Through this we agree to suspend disbelief and accept the novel as "gesturing towards" a recognisable or imaginable exterior world (*Structuralist* 193). If the referential data is inconsistent then it is difficult or impossible for us to compose such a world; if too much of it seems unrelated to plot, theme or character, then although we can recognise external references we have no means of organising them into a coherent whole and are left with "flawed or incomplete meanings" (*Structuralist* 193). Then we are forced "to read the text as an autonomous verbal object" (*Structuralist* 193). I would add the presence of a sense of place to Culler's list of components, because this, too, is an important means by which readers

construct a perceived or imagined extra-textual world. To a significant extent, these various means of construction are missing in *Trout
Fishing*. The book has no plot, no theme, no continuous cast of characters and no consistency of view; location shifts across time and
space and also from the plausibly real to the utterly surreal. What the
book appears to be seeking is the status of its equivalent in the art
world: a collage that is composed of fragments from and references
to the "real" world but which, as a whole, cannot be understood as a
representation of that world, but only as a self-referring object within
it. Further, the notion of what constitutes a text is extended to include
the printed surfaces beyond the book's chapters, including the front
cover. The physical/visual presence of the text is also emphasised,
along with its capacity for non-semantic signification. *Trout Fishing*,
therefore, is conceived as an aesthetic object with a material as well
as a literary place in the world.

Theme, plot, character, location and the transcending of genre

Most of *Trout Fishing*'s brief chapters can be read as self-contained
and they range from recollections of fishing trips, through vignettes
of contemporary bohemian life in San Francisco to recipes, imagi-
nary letters, tall tales and even a strange excursion into the world of
Jack the Ripper. Many critics, particularly earlier ones, have chosen
to treat this fragmentation as if it is a cryptic crossword clue or an
anagram. Something recognisably "novelistic" could be found if only
one looked hard enough. There seemed to be no plot, no study of
character or relationships, so surely there had to be a theme. The critic's job was to uncover it. For the most part, there has been agreement
on the answer: *Trout Fishing*'s theme is the fate of American ideal-
ism, the latter bound up with pastoral myths and moralistic notions
of the American Dream. The narrator's angling expeditions are interpreted as a symbolic search for a better, purer America.

There has been disagreement, though, about the spirit in which this
journey is undertaken. Is the narrator offering a lament, a satire, or a
neutral piece of reportage? For John Barber, Manfred Pütz and others
it is a lament. Barber, writing about Brautigan's work in general, says

that he "mourned the betrayal of the American Dream and promoted the search for a new American Eden" (*Annotated* 12). For Pütz, Brautigan is a secularised Transcendentalist, albeit in diluted form, and *Trout Fishing* a "search for the lost paradise". Even Marc Chénetier, who sees language itself as *Trout Fishing*'s primary concern, says that the book is "a lament for the destruction of the American Dream by a trivial culture" (40). Schmitz argues for satire, which would align *Trout Fishing* with *Confederate General*; the pastoral idyll has never existed except as a mythology generated by urban America and Brautigan, while attracted to the myth, is sufficiently sceptical to treat it ironically. On the other hand Edward Foster, among others, stresses the emotional neutrality of the narrative voice in Brautigan's fiction, which locates him as a dispassionate recorder of America's fallen state (Foster 51, 72, 74).

With the possible exception of Schmitz, who notes ambivalence in Brautigan's attitude, the problem with these critical accounts is that they impose a consistency of viewpoint on the text. Brautigan has provided a sky full of strange clouds in which too many critics insist that they can recognise the outline of a familiar face. They can point, for instance, to several passages that support the thesis that Brautigan is mourning a lost pastoral idyll, but unfortunately there are also some which contradict it. In support, there are chapters such as "The Last Time I Saw Trout Fishing in America" (TF 89–91), in which the narrator talks to a personification of the book's title. This personification, playing a similar timeless witness role to that of Tiresias in "The Waste Land", recalls seeing the American explorers, Meriwether Lewis and William Clark, arriving at the Great Falls of the Missouri River on their transcontinental expedition of 1803–1805. The narrator recalls his own childhood in the subsequent city of Great Falls, Montana, when, instead of discovering natural wonders, he discovers a Deanna Durbin movie, watches it seven times without knowing why, and remembers "a childhood fancy" that the river would one day look "just like a Deanna Durbin movie – a chorus girl who wanted to go to college or she was a rich girl or they needed money for something or she did something" (TF 90). He also recalls such sombre experiences as an empty cinema, a freezing winter, and living in a cheap hotel room. Contrastingly, Trout Fishing in America's recollections of an unspoilt landscape are infused with nostalgia and expressed in Biblical cadences:

> "I remember the day Lewis discovered the falls. They left their camp at sunrise and a few hours later they came upon a beautiful plain and on the plain were more buffalo than they had ever seen before in one place.
>
> "They kept on going until they heard the faraway sound of a waterfall and saw a distant column of spray rising and disappearing. They followed the sound as it got louder and louder. After a while the sound was tremendous and they were at the great falls of the Missouri River. It was about noon when they got there.
>
> [...]
>
> "No, I don't think Lewis would have understood it if the Missouri River had suddenly begun to look like a Deanna Durbin movie, like a chorus girl who wanted to go to college," Trout Fishing in America said. (TF 91)

Yet to set against such nostalgia for an assumed Golden Age, we find passages in which mythologising the past is firmly rejected. In "Knock on Wood (Part One)" (TF 3), Trout Fishing in America recalls an early generation of Americans, "people with three-cornered hats fishing in the dawn", not with nostalgia but "with particular amusement", as if they are figures of fun rather than heroes of greater days. Similarly, when the narrator describes the life of a pioneer, Charles Hayman, it is not a Daniel Boone figure who emerges but something much more like the parodic pioneering of Lee Mellon in *Confederate General.* Hayman lives in a shack, does not hunt or farm and scrounges a living out of odd jobs. The narrator calls him an "old fart" and a "half-assed pioneer" (TF 27). The pioneering past is similarly demythologised when the narrator comes across an empty shack on a fishing trip. He does not muse on the instructive lives of the people who might have lived there in better, simpler times. Instead he has the shack's outhouse deliver an address dismissing the notion that the buildings hold any symbolic value: " 'There's no mystery here. That's why the door's open.' " The narrator's response is equally unromantic: " 'Fuck you,' I said to the outhouse. 'All I want is a ride down the river'" (TF 7). Yearning and a sense of loss are certainly present in *Trout Fishing*, but so is a tough-minded rejection of such sentiments. They co-exist, cautiously circling each other.

A related notion to the supposed theme of nostalgia for better days is that of the narrator being on a doomed quest for this lost, or illusory, pastoral idyll. This is symbolised, Malley and others argue, by the fact that his fishing trips all end in disappointment. Malley interprets them as symbolising a fruitless search for a life "of absolute freedom and independence" (147), which would resonate with the unsuccessful escape to nature of Jesse, the narrator of *Confederate General*. Certainly the expeditions often end in frustration. Yet the narrator does actually manage to land a good many trout in the course of the book and several times expresses satisfaction with his experience. In "The Lake Josephus Days" (TF 78–79), for instance, he catches his legal limit within an hour and talks of "all the excitement of good fishing" (TF 78). As for a failure to find unspoilt wilderness, symbol of an unspoilt America, when the narrator does come across some untamed country, at Tom Martin Creek (TF 19), he finds it a little too wild for his liking. Further, when he is looking for a model of the Good Life, he finds it not among homesteaders, mountain men, hunters, hikers or fishermen but in the relationship between a man and a woman living in a sleazy San Francisco hotel. In one of the very few such judgements in the book, he remarks: "They had a good world going for them" (TF 69).

Such urban settings are an important feature of the book, interspersed among the chapters involving camping, fishing, or other country activities. The ones most cited as underpinning an alleged theme of pastoral yearning are those set wholly or partly in San Francisco. These have been characterised by Kenneth Seib and others as representing a fallen world, an urban perversion of the Eden conjured by Trout Fishing in America's memories of Lewis and Clark. Arguably, the key chapters here are "The Shipping of Trout Fishing in America Shorty to Nelson Algren" (TF 45–47) and "The Cleveland Wrecking Yard" (TF 102–107). Trout Fishing in America Shorty is a legless, belligerent drunk. He is seen by Malley (150), Seib and others as a skid-row antithesis of the pristine, pastoral values represented by Trout Fishing in America. Yet Joseph Mills notes an interesting fact about Shorty. He tells children that he is crippled because " 'The trout chopped my legs off in Fort Lauderdale' " (TF 45). Who or what is "the trout"? Trout are an ambiguous symbol in *Trout Fishing* but most often they seem to be part of an idealistic/ idealised notion of the American Dream, and to demonstrate by their elusiveness how unobtainable that dream can be. There might also be a more particular identification with Trout Fishing in America's elegiac manifestation, because Shorty refers to "the" trout rather than "a" trout. In either case, the same point is made as in *Confederate General*: the American Dream and pastoral redemption are illusions. Shorty makes the mistake of believing in them and therefore, as Mills argues, "[Shorty] has been crippled by the myth." (58) Rather than the city blighting pastoral America, it is the city's pastoral mythologising that has created the urban cripple.

"The Cleveland Wrecking Yard" is possibly the funniest chapter in a frequently funny book. The narrator begins with a long digression and then he slips in this sentence, delivered in the same matter-of-fact tone: "My own experience with the Cleveland Wrecking Yard began two days ago when I heard about a used trout stream they had on sale out at the Yard." (TF 103) A used trout stream for sale in a wrecking yard? While we are digesting this, the narrator dives off into a further digression before returning to the fantastical notion of a second-hand trout stream. He arrives at the yard and sees a big sign:

USED TROUT STREAM FOR SALE.

MUST BE SEEN TO BE APPRECIATED. (TF 104)

A salesman asks if he can help:

> "Yes," I said. "I'm curious about the trout stream you have for sale. Can you tell me something about it? How are you sell-ing it?"
>
> "We're selling it by the foot length. You can buy as little as you want or you can buy all we've got left. A man came in here this morning and bought 563 feet. He's going to give it to his niece for a birthday present," the salesman said.
>
> "We're selling the waterfalls separately of course, and the

trees and birds, flowers, grass and ferns we're also selling extra. The insects we're giving away free with a minimum purchase of ten feet of stream." (TF 104)

The narrator gets directions to the stream: " 'It's stacked in lengths. You can't miss it. The waterfalls are upstairs in the used plumbing department'" (TF 105).

The whole Twain-inflected tall tale can be read as a satire of commerce's greedy exploitation of the environment. This would align it with concerns in a *Revenge* story, "The Gathering of a Californian" (RL 16). Even a trout stream, iconic symbol of pastoral values, site of the purifying and regenerative ritual of fishing, is commoditised, stacked in a shed and sold by the foot. It does not even have the status of a brand because it has no name. Interpreting the text as a satire, however, involves making judgements that are not present in the text. The narrative voice is neutral, perhaps playfully tongue-in-cheek, rather than outraged, sorrowful or scornful. Kathryn Hume, commenting on interpretations of Brautigan that claim to detect a clear authorial point of view, says that his observations are mostly "empty of judgement"; however, critics have chosen to "pour their own reactions" into Brautigan's "carefully constructed voids". Yet even if we accept the chapter as satire, the point is that, as usual, *Trout Fishing* does not offer us a stable viewpoint. "Wrecking Yard" may satirise urban commercialism's exploitation of the pastoral world but, as mentioned earlier, the only people in the book who are said to have a "good world going for them" are a couple who are very much a part of that urban world. As in *Confederate General*, contentment is about a state of mind not a location, and there is no clear and consistent viewpoint that sets up a dichotomy of Degraded City v. Pastoral Idyll. Instead, as with its other supposed themes, *Trout Fishing* offers only conflicted meanings which act like differing signposts, each pointing to the same place and claiming to know its name.

Most critics who say that *Trout Fishing* has a theme present no evidence, merely asserting that this is so. Gair is an exception, putting forward a credible case for the presence of a theme, so his argument deserves separate consideration. His case rests on three elements in the book: the focus placed on Benjamin Franklin in the first chapter, the book's structure (or lack of it) and the role of the "character", Trout Fishing in America. Gair points to Brautigan's description of Franklin's statue, and an allusion to his famous *Autobiography*, and sees these as standing for ordered, mainstream values: a materialist vision of the American Dream in which status, wealth and fame can be achieved by anyone if they apply themselves rigorously. However, whereas Franklin and his book offer orderly, chronological narratives of conventional achievement, Brautigan "leaps from one anecdote to another, seemingly at random, celebrating particular moments for themselves rather than seeing them as points on a path [to conventional success]" (*Counterculture* 157). Further, whereas the *Autobiography* traces an identifiable person's classic rise from rags to riches, Trout Fishing in America, whom Gair sees as Brautigan's protagonist, "is a fragmented assemblage of many 'characters' whose story illustrates an inversion of the usual markers of progression and results in withdrawal from conventional American life" (157). Therefore *Trout Fishing* constitutes a rejection of Franklin's life and works and, by extension, a critique of the mainstream values which they represent.

Nevertheless, although *Trout Fishing* may seem like a random scatter of anecdotes, it is actually a coherent reading experience, as I shall argue later in this chapter. A collage-based organising principle can be found and therefore this book is not some anarchic refutation of good order but the establishment or rediscovery of a different kind of order. Some rather more conventional, Franklinesque ordering principles can be found in Brautigan's working life. Like Franklin, he worked hard and meticulously to achieve his ambition. In the years covered by this study (1957–1969) he produced seven books of poetry, four novels and the short stories which constitute *Revenge*; *Trout Fishing* went through multiple revisions and Abbott says that his friend "worked his prose over and over to get the simplicity and clarity he loved." (*Downstream* ix); Brautigan also liked to be heavily involved in all aspects of publication, including marketing. Once more like Franklin, he was an autodidact who rose from disadvantaged obscurity to celebrity and (relative) wealth. They may not be identical twins but they are a long way from polar opposites.

In answer to Gair's point about Trout Fishing in America, I would say that this assemblage is not a character at all. As argued later in the chapter, the title of Trout Fishing in America is applied to so many conflicting phenomena in the book that it ceases to signify anything other than itself. One manifestation, the timeless Tiresias-like figure, does say that he is quitting urbanised America for Alaska, but another is a rich gourmet, and a third is a skid row hotel. I see this as a strategy which resists our ability to connect coherently with the perceived world rather than a contribution to a theme drawn from that world.

Edward Foster is the only critic I am aware of who identifies a plot, or at least a sequential, episodic narrative, in *Trout Fishing*. He sees the book's fishing-trip chapters as a chronological axis, although he accepts that "this is only obliquely apparent" (55). However, although these fishing chapters are split between childhood/youth experiences and those as an adult, they do not follow a chronological sequence from youth to adulthood. More importantly, the chapters that involve fishing trips are significantly outnumbered by those that do not. Foster's response to this is to argue that the miscellaneous chapters are arranged thematically to complement or to contrast with those in the supposed axis (55). If chapters can be either complementary or non-complementary, yet still be thematically linked to the axis, then no conceivable chapter would be out of place. In fact, many of the chapters provide the kind of jarring disruption that Brautigan's mischievous digressions and self-subverting metaphors achieve, making disconnections rather than connections. For instance, the three chapters following the first one (TF 3–7) tell us how the narrator was introduced to fishing, describe an unsuccessful childhood fishing trip and then move to an adult fishing expedition. Just as the opening of *Confederate General* leads us to expect a historical novel about the American Civil War, so these chapters seem to have established a pattern of strange trout-fishing yarns. But in the next chapter, "The Kool-Aid Wino" (TF 8–10), fishing disappears and we have a tale about a boyhood friend of the narrator who is able to get drunk on Kool-Aid. This is followed by a chapter called "Another Method of Making Walnut Catsup" (TF 11–12) which consists almost entirely of recipes. Such offerings are a series of non-sequiturs, further expressions of the liking for paratactical juxtapositions found throughout Brautigan's work. Here, as elsewhere, the text seems to be teasing our need for order and coherence.

Of course, one could argue that as *Trout Fishing* has no theme and no sequential narrative, we should simply treat it as a collection of short stories. But *Trout Fishing* is conceived and operates as an integrated artistic performance. The title page declares that it is a novel, and even if we baulk at that, it is certainly a single, extended work of fiction. Most individual chapters may be read as self-contained, but their full significance is only revealed by treating them as part of the whole. If we read a chapter that presents only one manifestation of Trout Fishing in America, we miss the point that there are many contradictory manifestations within the book, and therefore that the title is ultimately a signifier that points only at itself. If we read only a chapter which seems to endorse a theme of pastoral yearning, or urban degradation, we miss the point that other chapters subvert those meanings. Many of the chapters that act as non-sequiturs in *Trout Fishing* – "Another Recipe for Walnut Catsup" or "The Mayonnaise Chapter", for instance – would have no worthwhile meaning at all, either for writer or reader, outside of their subversive role within the structure. The whole depends upon its parts, and the parts depend upon the whole.

Just as there is no thematic or narrative construction, so there is no construction of character – at least, not in the traditional sense of producing carefully considered representations whose experiences and development we can follow. The book's title is personified as the Tiresias figure described earlier, but the name is also bestowed on a wide range of other phenomena, from Trout Fishing in America Shorty to a low-life hotel and a rich gourmet. The effect of this is to leave us uncertain about whom or what "Trout Fishing in America" might be. The narrator is nameless, as in *Watermelon* and *The Abortion*, and so is the woman who appears with him in several chapters. Her relationship to the narrator is unknown and she is given neither dialogue nor any description. Neither do we learn much about the narrator. He expresses few judgements and, as I have argued, when opinions are present they are liable to be subverted elsewhere. Sometimes he is a first-person narrator who claims to have participated in what he records; at other times he is a third-person narrator of events that he cannot have experienced; sometimes, as in "The Mayonnaise Chapter" (TF 112), which consists entirely of a letter neither sent nor received by him, he seems to have disappeared altogether. There is no stable sense of self. For all we know, there may be more than one narrator. Meanwhile, other characters in *Trout Fishing* disappear almost as soon as they emerge.

Like the characters, locations come and go without being able to establish themselves. Various fishing streams and hill or forest settings are noted but rarely returned to. San Francisco makes some ghostly appearances, but locations also range across time and space from Victorian London in "The Mayor of the Twentieth Century" (TF 48) to contemporary Mooresville, Indiana, in "Prologue to Grider Creek" (TF 13), to childhood Portland, Oregon (TF 4–5), and on to Mexico (TF 80), New York (TF 76–77) and Great Falls, Missouri, the latter in both the 19th-century and in the narrator's childhood (TF 89–91). In a significant number of chapters the setting is irrelevant because the focus is on events, as in "The Kool-Aid Wino", and the location is barely mentioned. Other chapters have no location in the conventional sense, consisting of "external" texts, such as letters, which are either found objects or imagined ones. Where a location is evoked, it is frequently difficult to construct a sense of its presence because so little information is given. In "The Towel" (TF 86), for instance, the narrator tells us that he has been travelling from Lake Josephus and "down the road from Seafoam" and that he and his family have stopped for a drink. As so often, the narrator's eye is drawn to a text rather than the natural world. In this case it is a memorial to plane-crash victims, and while the setting is ignored other than being vaguely noted as "forest", the text on the monument is transcribed in full, taking up six lines of type. This detailed textual focus again reflects the fact that it is the landscapes of language that Brautigan wishes to explore and record. So it is that when he does come to describe a location, he frequently uses metaphors that leave us with a strong sense of performative language but no sense of place; bizarre or dissonant comparative terms disrupt our construction of meaning. In "Trout Death by Port Wine" (TF 29–32), a creek is compared to a department store, with the narrator catching three trout "in the lost and found department"; he later describes the stream as "crashing through the children's toy section" (TF 31). We are conscious that a role reversal is at play: locations are used to construct a linguistic landscape rather than language being used to create a sense of place. It is a romance of names not locations that Brautigan is celebrating, as made explicit in this passage:

> We left Little Redfish for Lake Josephus, *traveling along the good names* [my italics] – from Stanley to Capehorn to Seafoam to the Rapid River, up Float Creek, past the Greyhound Mine and then to Lake Josephus, and a few days after that up the trail to Hell-diver Lake.... (TF 78)

This is the kind of imaginative transcendence that Brautigan had shown himself capable of developing since his early poetry-prose hybrids, and many critics have noted the important role that the imagination plays in *Trout Fishing*. Some, however, tend to see that role as harnessed to a supposed theme within the narrative. Most popular of these notions is one that I have traced through the poetry to *Watermelon* and *Confederate General*: the imagination as an escape from unacceptable reality. Thomas Hearron presents one version of this. "The novel's theme," he argues, "much like that of Wordsworth's *The Prelude*, is the development of the power of the imagination ... [as] a way of escaping to nature even in the midst of a city" (30). Barber presents a similar case (*Annotated* 12). Hearron identifies "The Kool-Aid Wino" (TF 8–10) as important in expressing this theme of imaginative release. The "wino" is a childhood friend of the narrator who is able to transform his perception of life by treating Kool-Aid as a mind-altering substance. The narrator says: "He created his own Kool-Aid reality and was able to illuminate himself by it." (TF 10) Certainly the imagination can be seen as a means of escape here, but as so often, *Trout Fishing* also proposes a conflicting thesis: in this case, imagination as a burden. As in *Watermelon*, to imagine too much can be to hope too much, and so to invite disappointment. Thus, in "The Surgeon" (TF 71–72), the narrator meets a man who has imagined his ideal trout-fishing site in terms that equate it with an idealised vision of America. The power of his imagination can only lead to disappointment, the text suggests, because America is "often only a place in the mind" (TF 72).

For the imagination as an unqualified source of positive transcendence, we must look to the structure and language of *Trout Fishing,* not to events recorded within its various narratives. Brooke Kenton Horvath argues that it is these qualities that constitute the imagination's escape (439). Following his general approach to Brautigan, he associates the imaginative transcendence with a symbolic escape from death or fears of death, which would align it with *Watermelon* and *Confederate General.* Hicks (158) and Chénetier (31–32) make a similar connection between mortal fears and Brautigan's attitude to the act of writing. Here, however, it is the literal escape achieved that I want to explore rather than any suggested symbolic one. That literal escape is from the conventions of fictive discourse, and thus from the means by which readers connect a literary text to a perceived or imaginable reality. *Trout Fishing* contains multiple narratives and most of these can make some kind of extra-textual connection for us, however disrupted it may be. But taken together, their lack of narrative continuity and thematic links, their inconsistent viewpoints, and the absence of character and a sense of place leave us disconnected. Hence, Klinkowitz can say that "*Trout Fishing* is less about philosophical matters than it is, quite simply, about itself" (*American 1960s* 44). Chénetier agrees, saying that "real world" themes can be found but that "Recourse to the referent does not provide an analysis; little advantage is gained from comparing the literary experience with 'reality'" (42). Brautigan, he argues, wants to revivify the written word from the deadening influence of convention and the weight of so many past texts. He says:

> Brautigan is a writer concerned with defying language's fixities and points of reference; indeed, I believe all his books are motivated by one central concern and activated by one central dialectic: they are driven by an obsessive interrogation of the fossilization and fixture of language, and by a counter-desire to free it from stultification and paralysis. (21)

Brautigan ends the text with a radical yet simple expression of that desire. In the penultimate chapter, the narrator tells us that he has always wanted to write a book ending with the word "mayonnaise". In the final chapter he does so, but in a seemingly irrelevant letter which misspells the word as "mayonaise". The misspelling is deliberate because it appears in subsequent editions.[1] Brautigan is demonstrating the freedom of his artistic imagination not only to end the book with a final non-sequitur, but to impose or allow an errant spelling.

The role of language and tone of voice

All of the key Brautigan mannerisms found in the books already discussed can be found, too, in *Trout Fishing* – and often in concentrated form. Idiosyncratic use of metaphoric language abounds, there are complex layers of intertextuality, surreal juxtapositions and events are common, ambiguity is almost a default mode, baffling digressions and omissions are frequent, and the tone of voice is typically dissonant. All these elements combine to heighten the sense of disconnection from "the real" produced by the book's structure.

As in all Brautigan's output, the self-subverting metaphor is the most extreme use of metaphoric language, and the device is more common in *Trout Fishing* than in any other Brautigan book. The chapter called "The Hunchback Trout" (TF 55–57) is a classic example, and also features some other disorientating staples of Brautigan's poetry and prose: the extended metaphor, disconnection through digression and omission, and the development of a comparative term into a new reality. The chapter introduces a self-subverting metaphor almost from the start:

> The creek was made narrow by little green trees that grew too close together. The creek was like 12,845 telephone booths in a row with high Victorian ceilings and all the doors taken off and all the backs of the booths knocked out.
>
> Sometimes when I went fishing in there, I felt just like a telephone repairman, even though I did not look like one. I was only a kid covered with fishing tackle, but in some strange way

---

1   Loewinsohn, according to Hortsberg, says that the letter is one of Brautigan's "found objects" – it had been used as a bookmark in a volume being read by Brautigan in a second-hand bookshop (*Jubilee* 174).

by going in there and catching a few trout, I kept the telephones in service. I was an asset to society. (TF 55)

We are told that the smaller trout are "perfect pan size for local calls" while the bigger ones are fine for long distance connections (TF 55); developing the repairman simile, the narrator tells us that the creek "was where I punched in. Leaving my card above the clock, I'd punch out again when it was time to go home" (TF 56). Then the telephone booth comparison is extended and turned into an actuality before being mixed with other strange disjunctive comparisons, and then temporarily abandoned as successive levels of digression are explored. By the end of the passage, so many alternative images/realities have been proposed that we are reminded of the multiple endings of *Confederate General*, denied any single, coherent vision, and have been taken very far from the narrative function of the chapter, which is to record a fishing trip:

> I waded about seventy-three telephone booths in. I caught two trout in a little hole that was like a wagon wheel. It was one of my favorite holes, and always good for a trout or two.
>
> I always like to think of that hole as a kind of pencil sharpener. I put my reflexes in and they came back out with a good point on them.
>
> ....The two trout lay in my creel covered entirely by green ferns, ferns made gentle and fragile by the damp walls of the telephone booths.
>
> The next good place was forty-five telephone booths in. The place was at the end of a run of gravel, brown and slippery with algae. The run of gravel dropped off and disappeared at a little shelf where there were some white rocks.
>
> One of the rocks was kind of strange. It was a flat white rock. Off by itself from the other rocks, it reminded me of a white cat I had seen in my childhood.
>
> That cat had fallen or been thrown off a high wooden sidewalk that went along the side of a hill in Tacoma, Washington. The cat was lying in a parking lot below.
>
> The fall had not appreciably helped the thickness of the cat, and then a few people had parked their cars on the cat. Of course,

that was a long time ago and the cars looked different from the way they look now.

You hardly see those cars any more. They are the old cars. They have to get off the highway because they can't keep up.

That flat white rock off by itself from the other rocks reminded me of that dead cat come to lie there in the creek, among 12,845 telephone booths. (TF 56–57)

Connections are suggested between the images presented, but the fragments refuse to cohere because the means for constructing those connections do not exist or have been omitted. The trout stream, vandalised telephone booths, a wagon wheel, a pencil sharpener, old cars and a dead cat seem to be linked only in and by the consciousness of the writer. Their paratactical juxtaposition mimics, at a micro level, the juxtaposition of the chapters, underpinning the latter's role in disconnecting the text as a whole from exterior reference. The initial self-subverting metaphor, comparing a tree-lined creek to 12,845 door-less, backless telephone booths with "high Victorian ceilings," supports this disconnection by failing to construct a single, coherent image. The majority of the 47 chapters have at least one such metaphor, and even when a Brautigan comparison does provide some kind of a connection between its terms, it usually has the dissonant strangeness of a surrealist painting. Chénetier notes how Brautigan's metaphors "wrench the reader's attention away from the apparent subject and destabilize the system of reference" (43). Abbott emphasises the element of play in this approach, a quality noted in *The Pill*, *Confederate General* and some *Revenge* stories: "He believed in the magic and spirit of play and worked very hard to get that quality in his writing" (*Downstream* 29). Charles Russell stresses the way in which Brautigan and other innovative writers reflect a sense of language's tenuous authority as a means of constructing meaning. "Language is silence in disguise," he says, and a metaphor can have "reference only to itself as an activity of mind against a dimension of mindlessness that it cannot contain or define" (350). Small wonder, then, that Brautigan should choose metaphors that "lead toward little more than themselves" (355). His images, Russell points out, "are always unmaking themselves, calling themselves into question, or being unpredictably dropped" (354).

Even more than *Confederate General, Trout Fishing* does not simply allude to other texts, real and imagined, but is constructed from them. By my count, there are 115 direct textual or authorial allusions in *Trout Fishing*'s 112 pages, many of them lengthy quotations. Virtually half of its chapters have as their focus, or as a significant factor, one or more texts, the act of writing, or a writer. Five of these chapters consist wholly or substantially of exterior texts – or, rather, texts that are presented as being exterior, because some are invented. Hemingway, Byron, Kafka and Nelson Algren are among the writers mentioned by name. As well as these direct references there is a plethora of indirect ones in which the style or content of other texts is evoked. The usual stylistic debts to the likes of Twain, Hemingway and Brautigan's poetic influences can be discerned, and critics have also uncovered various parodic references to literary works. Typical of these is the epitaph presented by Brautigan in "Trout Fishing on the Bevel" (TF 20–21), which takes up half a page:

Sacred

To the Memory

of

John Talbot

Who at the Age of Eighteen

Had His Ass Shot Off

In a Honky-Tonk

November 1, 1936

This Mayonnaise Jar

With Wilted Flowers In It

Was Left Here Six Months Ago

By His Sister

Who Is In

The Crazy Place Now. (TF 21)

On the face of it, this is a blackly comic invention of Brautigan's with no intentional connection to any other text. But Tanner (*City of Words* 414) and Stull (70) point out that it is actually a parody of an epitaph appearing in the seventh chapter of Melville's *Moby Dick*, on a tablet also erected by the sister of a deceased person. It reads, in part: "... JOHN TALBOT / Who, at the age of eighteen, was lost overboard, / Near the Isle of Desolation, off Patagonia, / *November* 1st, 1836...." Chénetier points to parody as a defining characteristic of Brautigan's use of allusion. Intertextuality is inevitable so one might as well exaggerate it and have irreverent fun with it rather than suffer preceding texts as a dead weight. Writing of Brautigan's general approach to fiction, Chénetier says: "Everywhere the remains of past texts are evoked and derided, through pastiche, parody or pun" (34). The sources of direct quotation are an eclectic mix, but tend to be from utilitarian usage rather than from literary works. Often they are wholly or partly fictitious. Sometimes, as with letters supposedly written by Trout Fishing in America, their fictitious nature is clear. Equally often it is difficult or impossible to distinguish between these and authentic found objects.

The narrator's tone of voice is another important factor in subverting our construction of meaning. With everyday occurrences, the tone suggests that remarkable events are happening; when events truly are remarkable, the tone suggests the everyday; when we should be appalled or disgusted, the tone tends to be neutral or even playful, as here, where the narrator describes having sex in a pool of slime and dead fish:

> We played and relaxed in the water. The green slime and the dead fish played and relaxed with us and flowed out over us and entwined themselves about us.
>
> .... I remember a dead fish floated under her neck. I waited for it to come up on the other side, and it came up on the other side.
>
> Worsewick was nothing fancy.
>
> Then I came, and just cleared her in a split second like an airplane in the movies, pulling out of a nosedive and sailing over the roof of a school.
>
> My sperm came out into the water, unaccustomed to the light, and instantly it became a misty, stringy kind of thing and swirled out like a falling star, and I saw a dead fish come forward and float into my sperm, bending it in the middle. His eyes were stiff like iron. (TF 43–44)

One result of this narrative voice is to set up a tension between what is being described and the language used to describe it. Consequently, dissonance is created, uncertainty about the narrator's reliability is emphasised and ambiguity emerges about how we should interpret the text, once more complementing the structure's disconnection from signification of an external world.

An aesthetic artefact

The materiality of *Trout Fishing* is inescapable, and Brautigan deals with this as he deals with other inevitable factors such as the indeterminacy of literary texts and their dependence on preceding texts: he gleefully exploits the situation through dramatisation. *Trout Fishing* is consciously presented as an integrated aesthetic object, thus expanding the semantic field's aspirations of self-containment into the material world as the text becomes part of an artefact whose printed surfaces are bound together not only physically but conceptually. In this, Brautigan is developing an interest first found in his juvenilia and continued through the early poetry published in San Francisco.

The title page of *Trout Fishing* tells us that what we are about to read is a novel. Therefore we are expecting prose. Two further preliminary pages offer a list of chapter titles, another element we might expect in a work of prose. However, when we actually reach the formal text, its lay-out immediately runs counter to expectation. As in so much of Brautigan's fiction, it has many of the visual qualities of poetry. Indeed, the majority of the 47 chapters are no more than two pages long, and are frequently much shorter than that; they repeatedly open up unexpected spaces through their brevity and by frequent use of paragraphs that are no more than a sentence or so in length. They might be a series of Whitmanesque poems, or part of a serial poem by Spicer. Inserted texts from notices, inscriptions and the like are an obsession and they, too, open up space and disrupt the expected shape of the prose. The result is a text which, in many chapters, appears to operate visually across the borders of genre, another prose-poetry hybrid. This follows the pattern established through detailed use of language; in this, the minimalist prose of Hemingway and the tall-tales prose of Twain are mingled with poetry's rhythmic patterns and metaphoric language.

One consequence of introducing some of the visual characteristics of verse into prose is that it disorientates us, reinforcing the subversion of expectations performed by structure and language. It also counters the referential role of text, drawing attention to its visual patterning, rather than to patterns of semantic meaning, just as structure and language work to sever connections to "the real". Of course, each character in a line of text is itself a piece of visual patterning and signifies graphically as well as semantically. When Brautigan was producing mimeographed broadsheets, no choice of typeface was possible. Mimeographing involved making a stencil from the original typescript, so the typeface would be whatever was on the typewriter. The standard typewriter face simply needed to be clear and robust, and although the result was serviceable it was aesthetically unappealing and could be hard on the eyes over long stretches. Publishers tended to avoid it. *Trout Fishing*'s first edition, however, chooses to use a typeface which actually mimics that of a typewriter. Mills comments on its crudeness and suggests that its simulation of typewritten text is "an attempt to convey a sense of immediacy of experience" (25–26). That is possible, and a simulated immediacy is certainly characteristic of performative texts such as this. But what is certain is that the typeface calls attention to the physical presence of the text and individualises its appearance. This awareness of the text's materiality is heightened by the use of underscores to indicate what would normally be italicised titles of books, films etc. Again, this mimics a typewritten text; typewriters tended to offer only roman (upright) faces and therefore a typescript submitted for publication would use underscores to indicate italics. Because *Trout Fishing* is so given to textual allusion, book titles provide plenty of opportunities for underscoring – some sixty throughout the text's 112 pages. Effectively, through its typography, *Trout Fishing* is presenting itself in manuscript form. Preserving the integrity of the text has involved retaining its graphic as well as its semantic qualities.

This concept is well expressed by Gass, who says of Rilke that it was very important for him "to send a copy of the finished poem in his beautiful hand to somebody because *that was* the poem, not some printed imitation" (LeClair). The ideal is that of the medieval codex, which was always an original; its hand-crafting ensured that even if a precise visual copy was intended it could never be achieved. At the time *Trout Fishing* was published, San Francisco had developed a new art form, the psychedelic poster, which advertised rock concerts and other gatherings. The lettering of the posters explodes in swirling, curvaceous, hallucinatory forms that can be seen as simulating some of the visual experiences of drug trips. In their own way, they are as focused on the visual qualities and possibilities of text as any illuminated manuscript. Brautigan's own mimeographed output placed him in a similar position to that of the poster artists. The finished product was a facsimile of the typescript and the fact that Brautigan was frequently responsible for providing or commissioning illustrations, pasting pages together and even distributing his work, further heightened this sense of individualisation and a direct connection with readers.

This, then, is the tradition which is being tapped into by *Trout Fishing* – a tradition of texts in which individualisation is achieved, in part, through a stress on the visual possibilities of written language and which, therefore, in reproduction, seeks a faithfulness not only to the semantic field of the original but also to its graphic field. In choosing this route, *Trout Fishing* is not only attempting to represent itself as an individualised entity rather than a mass produced commodity but once more calling attention to its own artifice: the unexpected format emphasises the existence of such formats. One way in which *Trout Fishing* deviates from the practice of the poster artists, however, is that its text is not a facsimile of an original but a simulation – and not even a simulation of the original, one suspects, but of typewriter script as a genre. Neither is the lettering aesthetically pleasing, as it is in the codices and posters. Its design draws attention to itself by its very inappropriateness. So in this respect, too, *Trout Fishing* differs from the codices and posters. It presents us with a parody of the manuscript/poster tradition.

The same mischievous approach is evident in the treatment of elements that would not normally be considered part of the text – the book's cover and the pages preceding the opening chapter. For instance, the opening sentence of the text immediately integrates the cover photograph into its discourse:

> The cover for <u>Trout Fishing in America</u> is a photograph taken late in the afternoon, a photograph of the Benjamin Franklin statue in San Francisco's Washington Square.

This opening alerts us to the cover as a significant factor and is likely to make us want to return to it. If we do, we will find that the narrator's description of the photograph will not tally with what we see. The photograph's primary focus is Brautigan and a seated muse rather than Franklin's statue, but neither the author nor his companion is mentioned. As Seib points out, this omission amounts to a pun on the word "cover" in the chapter title, because what follows is a hiding place or disguise for the narrator/author and his friend. This discrepancy between text and cover is an immediate and literally graphic way of establishing the narrator's unreliability and penchant for omission. This, in turn, points to a tendency in the book not to *make* sense but to unmake it. Abbott calls the cover shot the first scene in the book (*Downstream* 160). I would call it the first chapter because that stresses the continuity of signification in *Trout Fishing*, whether graphic or semantic.

This textual role of the cover is the single most striking example of *Trout Fishing*'s status as a graphic-semantic hybrid (just as it is a prose-poetry hybrid). A stress on hybridity is present throughout, of course, created by the emphasis placed on the non-semantic qualities of the printed word. But integrating the cover into the opening of the text is a typically theatrical stroke that immediately and dramatically foregrounds the importance of the non-semantic. What is more, by making the cover of the book the subject of the nominal first chapter of the text, a powerful statement is made about *Trout Fishing*: it is a project that seeks to unify text and context. There is the formal text, but there is also an extended text.

Moving from the cover to the title page, we find a second example of an element from this extended text that is essential to understanding *Trout Fishing*. As pointed out earlier, the page designates the work as a novel. Once we are told that this is the book's chosen genre, we read it as such and thus experience its almost total subversion of that genre's conventions. Brautigan states, or allows it to be stated, that he intends it to be a single prose fiction, a unified reading experience. The presentation of the type on this page gives further clues to how we should interpret *Trout Fishing*. The book's title, drawn by Brautigan, is playfully looped into the arcing shape of a trout leaping, or perhaps that of a bending rod and taut line as an angler tries to reel in a catch. This is not how one would expect a novel to introduce itself if it wanted to be taken seriously. It is more the kind of doodling embellishment that one might get in a light-hearted children's book. It also undercuts the iconography of the phrase, "Trout Fishing in America". The same mischievous irreverence is being exercised, the same avoidance or mockery of convention and tradition, as will be found throughout the book. Like the description of the book as a novel, it provides a signal that guides how we should read the text.

The next right-hand page of the extended text continues the playful tone. Brautigan's dedication of the book to Spicer and Loewinsohn is enclosed by a childish sketch of a grinning fish. Brautigan was very fond of creating such graffiti-like fish, and used one as the logo for his self-publishing venture, Carp Press. Loewinsohn makes the interesting suggestion that the drawing might be intended as a cartoon version not of a fish but of a whale, which would link it to *Moby Dick* and signal the irreverence, parody and intertextuality to come. The subsequent right-hand page – all the previous left-hand pages have been left blank – offers a list of contents that runs over onto the following page. It appears to be presented in the same spirit as the other two pages mentioned because, as Tony Tanner has pointed out, it is actually a mockery of such lists (*City of Words* 411). If the book was offering trout fishing tips and conventional reminiscences, as its title suggests it might, then a list of contents would be useful. But it is no such thing and, in any case, the chapter headings are frequently cryptic and/or bizarre so offer no hint of what might be found below them. Add to this the fact that Brautigan has divided his short novel into 47 chapters and you have a list of titles that straggles down the two contents pages like a free-form poem. The visual effect is complemented by the semantics. As with his poetry titles, Brautigan put a lot of thought into chapter headings. They frequently have an appealing ring to them even if their imagery makes them difficult or impossible to decode. "A Half-Sunday Homage to a Whole Leonardo da Vinci" (TF 108), for instance, is irresistibly intriguing.

Below the contents list are three lines that look and read as if they might be another poem. They could easily be one of Brautigan's haiku-esque offerings from *The Pill*. There is no title, however, and no attribution. The reader must assume that Brautigan is the author, but cannot be sure:

> There are seductions that should be
> in the Smithsonian Institute,
> right next to The Spirit of St. Louis.

The lines can be interpreted as a celebration of the private and seemingly trivial, a flattening of hierarchies in which a historic public event, in this case the first solo transatlantic flight, can be ranked alongside an obscure sexual conquest. But the statement is too cryptic for any certainty of interpretation. What is its purpose? Is it a key to understanding the text? If we could only "get" its message would all be revealed? Does it actually have a message, or is Brautigan just playing games again? In a further link between text and extended text, the famous flight is recalled in "The Towel" (TF 86). The narrator comes across a memorial in a forest to three men killed in a plane crash. There is a photograph on the memorial, and the narrator chooses to draw a connection between it and Charles Lindbergh, pilot of the *Spirit of St. Louis*:

> There was a man in the photograph who looked a lot like Charles A. Lindbergh. He had that same Spirit of St. Louis nobility and purpose of expression, except that his North Atlantic was the forests of Idaho.

Earlier in the preliminary pages we are presented with another puzzle. The first line of text once we are inside the cover comes in an unassumingly small typeface, centred high on an otherwise blank page, and is as follows: "Writing 14". Its significance is that *Trout Fishing* was the fourteenth work to be published by Donald Allen's Four Seasons imprint. In the small-print of the Delta edition's copyright and publication details, the Four Seasons Writing series is mentioned so, for those who read such things, there is a clue of sorts to the puzzling information's meaning. There is no such clue in the Houghton Mifflin collected edition. Unaided, I doubt if one in a thousand readers would be able to decode the message, particularly as they will almost certainly be encountering it in editions by subsequent publishers.

The only other printed surface before the formal text has a single line of type repeating the book's title; it is on the final right-hand page before the text's opening chapter and is conventionally displayed. In the Delta edition there are two other conventional pages of information, one listing Brautigan's other books and another giving the usual publication and copyright data. All three offer exactly what one would expect from pre-text pages and, through contrast, emphasise the unconventionality of the other pages. It is these individualised pages that stand out and therefore set the tone for the extended text. That tone is one that is at once complementary to that of the text and integrated with it. The book is an integrated system of printed surfaces that signifies its unified self-hood, its aspiration of self-containment, both graphically and semantically.

A final point about *Trout Fishing*, one which has not really attracted attention, is that although Brautigan is the prime mover, this is a collaborative enterprise. Several contemporaries point to Spicer's role as editor, and Ellingham and Killian say that Brautigan brought the manuscript to him "page by page, and the two men revised it as though it were a long serial poem" (Ellingham and Killian 223). Loewinsohn says that "Jack was able to get him to make changes" (Ellingham and Killian 223). Joanne Kyger says that Robin Blaser helped (Kyger 140) and Brautigan's first wife, Virginia, also claims to have been involved in editing, while confirming Spicer's involvement (Anderson). The crucial cover photograph was taken by Erik Weber, who says that the idea for the picture was also his (Barber *Archive*). The "Writing 14" line was most likely provided by the publisher.

However, none of this should detract from our estimation of Brautigan's achievement. We already know of his interest in books as physical-visual-semantic phenomena and one of his publishers,

Seymour Lawrence, tells us that he was "deeply involved in every detail and aspect of his books" and had a final say in "typography, design, jacket art" and even advertising copy (Hjortsberg *Jubilee* 19). The degree of involvement of the various "editors" is unknown, but the language is very much what we find in much of Brautigan's fiction. I suspect that the role of Spicer, the most frequently acknowledged editorial contributor, was to amplify the influence of Twain and the early Hemingway; between them, they help excise the sentimentality and whimsy that mar some of *The Pill*'s poetry. In doing so, they help to make Brautigan's prose the most effective vehicle for his poetic sensibility.

Chapter Seven: A long goodbye

Later work; the decline in reputation; the case for restoring it

Unable to label Brautigan's prose pieces satisfactorily, Robert Adams says that they may be beyond conventional categorisation and "go down in literary history as Brautigans." (24) You recognise "Brautigans" by their idiosyncratic combination of Hemingway minimalism and the flamboyantly surreal, their blurring of prose and poetry, their playfulness and intertextuality, and their frequent sense of language being explored as an end in itself, with any formal signification only a means to that end. The problem with such a distinctive style, however, is that it is a high-maintenance mode that requires copious amounts of re-invention to prevent new submissions from seeming stale and mannered. It was a problem that Brautigan did not really address. The late 1960s and early 1970s see further experimentation among his peers but, after *The Abortion*, Brautigan retreats into what looks suspiciously like a comfort zone. Genre parody was always a part of his fiction but, following the example of *The Abortion,* the next novels signal their self-reflexive interest in genre through their subtitles as Brautigan settles into a predominantly parodic mode that no longer pushes at boundaries. Most of the books are enjoyable, with plenty of good jokes and inventive use of language. Mostly, though, Brautigan is repeating himself.

The Hawkline Monster: A Gothic Western, is the first of these books, and very good of its kind. Two blackly comedic Wild West gunmen set out on a romance-style quest to save a damsel by slaying a monster in a remote mansion; they find that the monster, the damsel, and the mansion are very different from what they expected. The subsequent *Willard and his Bowling Trophies: a Perverse Mystery*, is slight, despite an amusing passage in which the hero engages apologetically in bondage. *Dreaming of Babylon: A Private Eye Novel 1942*, although highly entertaining, cannot avoid a sense of ambition lost, of a formula being applied, as a hapless version of a Chandler or Hammett private detective shambles around San Francisco in pursuit of a corpse. Between the latter two novels is a more ambitious offering, *Sombrero Fallout: a Japanese Novel*. It intertwines three stories told from different perspectives and deserves to be ranked with Brautigan's best work. The central conceits are that a story discarded by a heartbroken novelist carries on writing itself, and that a sombrero can land like some alien spacecraft and create havoc in a community. It is inventive, funny and poignant. Less convincing is 1979's *The Tokyo-Montana Express*, which is generally no more than a less successful version of *Revenge*, with vignettes from Japan, Montana and elsewhere. The tone of the final two books is that of *Revenge*'s more melancholy pieces. *So the Wind Won't Blow it All Away* ostensibly tells the tale of an accidental death caused by the narrator in childhood. It proceeds through repetition and long digressions which are profoundly irritating, unlike their 1960s' counterparts. *An Unfortunate Woman* is really about an unfortunate man, the author. It is in diary form and returns to the tone of the childhood short stories. The diary reveals Brautigan's life and mind unravelling as he moves manically from place to place. Knowing that this was Brautigan's last complete, extended work before he killed himself adds poignancy, but even without that knowledge the tense restraint of the prose makes this a powerful text. Brautigan also published a further three volumes of verse during the 1970s – *Rommel Drives on Deep into Egypt, Loading Mercury with a Pitchfork,* and *June 30th., June 30th*. The latter is the most interesting, conceptually, following the Japanese tradition of a traveller's tale told through collected verse. Elsewhere, the tone is similar to the later poems of *The Pill*, with *Rommel* taking brevity to new lengths, including four poems with titles but no text (RD 2, 27, 38, 78). The latter can seem like self-indulgent pranks; yet they are clearly a logical extension of Brautigan's life-long belief in the eloquence of omission.

By the time of his death in 1984, popular and academic interest in Brautigan was negligible. *An Unfortunate Woman* failed to find a publisher after two offers with low advances were rejected by Brautigan. It did not appear until ten years after his death – and then in a French edition, under a different title, translated by Chénetier.[1] No doubt American publishers had been deterred by the performance of *So the Wind*, which sold only 15,000 copies in the US (Boyer 6). The decline in popularity for this former best-seller began earlier, however. Abbott tells of Brautigan's dismay in touring universities to promote *Tokyo-Montana* and finding that he had declined from campus hero to "someone no longer even known by young readers" (*Downstream* 134). Some had lost interest before that. Steve Heilig remembers becoming "one of the guilty ones" who gave up on Brautigan "around the time of ... *The Hawkline Monster*" (122).

Writing not long before Brautigan's death, Chénetier bemoans the fact that the author had been critically discarded while Barthelme was lauded for producing equivalent work (17). He sees critical appraisal as being distorted by Brautigan's presentation as "the product-image-leader of the Woodstock-generation sensibility" (15). Once that sensibility became derided, Brautigan was easier for critics to dismiss and popular appeal also waned, even though he had never really been a hippie, and even though *Trout Fishing*'s first draft came years before the hippies existed. Abbott makes similar points to Chénetier and adds that Brautigan's status as a West Coast writer was a factor and so was his relative lack of education. The critical establishment was based in the east and had shown "open hostility" from the first (*Downstream* 147). They were academics, or academically trained, and published in critical journals and prestigious magazines. Brautigan had only a high school diploma (with grades towards the lower end of his class), and did not conceptualise his writing; outside of his books, the single most likely place to find his work was not in any literary publication but in the rock magazine, *Rolling Stone.*

With the appearance of *Trout Fishing* in Norton's anthology of post-modern writing, the "large critical desert" noted by Chénetier (19) seems to have shrunk somewhat. Yet as Gair points out in a 2012 essay on Brautigan, neglect is still widespread, with the writer

---

1   Brautigan. *Cahiers d'un Retour du Troie*. Trans. Marc Chénetier. Paris: Bourgois, 1994.

remaining "trapped within his epoch" ("Perhaps the Words" 5). If we turn first to *Revenge* as evidence of the injustice of this, we find sufficient successes to justify Malley's view that Brautigan is "a master of the short short story". The use of the surreal to infiltrate and ultimately take over a text is beautifully handled, as in "The Weather in San Francisco" (RL 31–32), and also skilfully and amusingly deployed as symbolism in stories such as "The Wild Birds of Heaven" (RL 38–41). Brautigan's greatest contribution, however, is the fusion of prose and poetry that creates short stories with much of the look, language and subject matter of lyric poetry. Any anthology of 20th-century American short stories is much the poorer without at least one example of what Brautigan was able to do with the form.

Then there is *Watermelon*, which Michael McClure believes to be Brautigan's "most perfect book" ("Ninety-One Things" 164). The novel has a broadly conventional structure but manages to achieve an extremely unusual effect by constructing a notion of iDEATH consciousness not only through description within the narrative but through a simulation of that consciousness in the texture of the language and in the structure. The dream-like flow of the prose-poetry can lead one to miss the fact that this is also a very careful exploration of the choices faced by those dealing with the brute facts of mortality without the consolation of religion. *Confederate General* has been discussed in the context of metafictional experiments of the time and is a particularly interesting contribution to that experimentation. It is uneven, but bold in its mixing of historical fact and fancy, of the past with the present, and in its satire of literary genres and American mythologies. The way in which it flaunts intertextuality is also striking, as is the way that, like *Watermelon*, its language builds a simulacrum of an important element within the narrative. Most striking of all are the infinite endings which undermine the narrative structure that Brautigan has built.

The Abortion is a subtly symbolic exploration of a writer's frustration with his chosen medium, and the library section is wonderfully inventive and well handled; but once the "action" moves beyond the library there is too much slackness for the novel as a whole to be put forward as an example of Brautigan's worth. That leaves us finally, and most importantly, with *Trout Fishing*. With this book, his first extended fiction, Brautigan produces one of the foremost innovatory American texts of its time. It seeks – and to a considerable degree achieves – overall independence from a referential role. Removal of crucial elements of conventional narrative discourse prevent us from being able to say what the book is "about", other than itself and other texts. It is a textual collage constructed, to a significant degree, from references to, or quotations from, other texts – and also from allusions to itself. The sense of disconnection is heightened by the emphasis on the text's graphical field and by its integration with the extended text, most notably the book's cover. This locates *Trout Fishing* as an integrated, consciously created material presence as well as a literary one, an aesthetic object drawing on the tradition of the codex and the psychedelic poster but, as so often with Brautigan, doing so parodically. It is also worth noting that *Trout Fishing*'s experimentalism does not come at the expense of accessibility, in sharp contrast to many or even most innovative writers. It answered or anticipated a call from critics including Susan Sontag, Fiedler and Barth for a non-elitist literature. Such critics helped provide the academic underpinning for what we have come to see as one of the characteristics of post-modern writing – a flattening of artistic hierarchies. In "The Literature of Replenishment", Barth calls for a move away from wilfully "difficult" art because "we really don't *need* more *Finnegan's Wakes* and *Pisan Cantos*, each with its staff of tenured professors to explain it to us" (177).

How distinctive is *Trout Fishing*'s contribution to American literature? Or, a more manageable question: how radical is its approach to narrative discourse compared to the previously-published work of Brautigan's American contemporaries? No list for comparison can be exhaustive and all lists are contentious. Mine is based on the standard Norton anthology, *Postmodern American Fiction*, supplemented by Jerome Klinkowitz's *Literary Disruptions* and *The American 1960s*. In the Norton book, the first section, "Breaking the Frame", contains extracts from writers seen as challenging the conventions of fiction. Brautigan is included (eccentrically, Barth is not, although he is represented in another section). Of these writers, those who produced extended fiction in the 1950s and/or the pre-*Trout Fishing* 1960s are Thomas Pynchon, William S. Burroughs, Donald Barthelme, Ishmael Reed, William H. Gass and Kurt Vonnegut. Klinkowitz acknowledges some of those and allows us to add Jerzy Kosinski, Steve Katz, Gilbert Sorrentino, Robert Coover and LeRoi Jones (later Amiri Baraka). I add John Barth to the list because his importance in developing innovative models in post-war American literature seems inarguable to me. This gives us the following list of pre-*Trout Fishing* titles:

> Barth: *The End of the Road* (1958), *The Floating Opera* (1956), *Giles Goat-Boy* (1966), *The Sot-Weed Factor* (1960)
>
> Barthelme: *Snow White* (1967)
>
> Burroughs: *Junky* (1953), *Naked Lunch* (1959), *Nova Express* (1964), *The Soft Machine* (1961), *The Ticket that Exploded* (1962)
>
> Coover: *The Origin of the Brunists* (1966)
>
> Gass: *Omensetter's Luck* (1966)
>
> Jones: *The System of Dante's Hell* (1965)
>
> Katz: *The Lestriad* (1962)
>
> Kosinski: *The Painted Bird* (1965)
>
> Pynchon: *The Crying of Lot 49* (1966), *V* (1963)
>
> Reed: *The Free-lance Pallbearers* (1967)
>
> Sorrentino: *The Sky Changes* (1966)
>
> Vonnegut: *Cat's Cradle* (1963), *God Bless You, Mr. Rosewater* (1965), *Mother Night* (1962), *Player Piano* (1952), *The Sirens of Titan* (1959)

Some of these books, such as Coover's *The Origin of the Brunists*, Gass's *Omensetter's Luck* and Vonnegut's *Player Piano*, are early pieces by writers who did not become structurally adventurous until later. Others, however, such as Barth's *The Sot-Weed Factor*, Pynchon's *The Crying of Lot 49* and, most strikingly, Barthelme's *Snow White*, have strong metafictional elements; nevertheless, they still employ conventions which direct us to a world beyond the text, however mischievously these conventions are used. Two of the least classifiable works are Katz's *The Lestriad* and Jones's *The System of*

Dante's Hell; both are compelling, maverick texts, and the latter's fragmented poetry-prose hybridity has many echoes of Brautigan. For all its ambiguity and disjunctive manner, however, *Dante* is a memoir and therefore performs a referential role, albeit through unconventional means. As for *The Lestriad*, its organising principle seems to be the irrational logic of dreams, with time, character, events and location shifting unpredictably. What anchors it to the "real world", however, is its strong sense of place (a decadent, violent, aimless New York) and its theme, as described in the publisher's preface, of "our very American need to find heroism within ourselves and those around us".

Burroughs probably comes closest to the disconnectedness of *Trout Fishing*. *Naked Lunch*, for instance, has no narrative axis; Burroughs tells us that we can begin the book anywhere we like (*Naked Lunch* 187). The text also differs between some editions, challenging our notions of a literary work as a stable entity. In Burroughs, too, we often find dashes rather than conventional punctuation separating short, stabbing statements, many of which seem to be non-sequiturs, while other statements trail away in ellipses. The ultimate assault on predetermined linguistic structures is the cut-up technique pioneered by Dada and first used by Burroughs in *Nova Express*; phrases from other publications are randomly juxtaposed to unmake or randomise meaning more thoroughly than anything in *Trout Fishing*. In Burroughs's approach, though, there is a political dimension absent in *Trout Fishing*. Burroughs saw language as a socio-political conditioning force employed by power elites, or what Burroughs refers to in *Nova Express* – and elsewhere, in broadly similar terms – as "the all-powerful boards and syndicates of the earth" (4). Not only text but film and sound recording are used to condition our perception of life. Burroughs pursues these themes from the perceived world through his texts. Therefore, like the other works on my list, the Burroughs novels do not eschew referentiality as thoroughly as *Trout Fishing*. In fact, given his desire to explore themes from the perceived world, referentiality is essential to Burroughs.

Neither does any of these novels show the same awareness of its materiality as *Trout Fishing*, with Barthelme's *Snow White*, published in the same year as *Trout Fishing*, probably coming closest. Slightly later, exuberant expressions of non-semantic signification come in Gass's novel, *Willie Masters' Lonesome Wife*, with its strong graphic focus, including the integration of photographs, and in Vonnegut's *Breakfast of Champions*, where the author's own sketches replace what would have been passages of descriptive prose. We also find radical experimentation with form in novels such as Raymond Federman's *Double or Nothing*, which varies its structuring principles throughout and in which we are told at the outset that we are not at the beginning of the story. But these post-date *Trout Fishing*. Nothing before it from the peer group of contenders matches its radical genre transcendence, its exploration of how far one can go to create an extended, self-referential fiction that integrates both a literary and a physical/visual aesthetic.

Trout Fishing alone should be enough to secure Brautigan's reputation, but to that can be added the inimitable nature of his general writing style – his "Brautigans" – the achievements of *Confederate General* and *Watermelon*, a significant number of *Revenge*'s stories, and, from the later work, *Sombrero Fallout* and *An Unfortunate Woman*.

Throughout his fiction, Brautigan demonstrated a fascination with memorial texts so it seems fitting to end with one – invented, of course, as were so many of Brautigan's:

> Somewhere in this discarded pile of caftans, tie-dye tops and smiling Indian gurus lies the not-quite-dead reputation of Richard Brautigan. Please remove and resuscitate.

Works Cited

Abbott, Keith. *Downstream from* Trout Fishing in America. Santa Barbara, CA: Capra, 1989.

———. "In The Riffles." *Essays.* Barber.

———. "Introduction: Young, Desperate, and in Love." *Edna Webster Collection.* By Brautigan: xi–xvii.

Adams, Robert. "Brautigan Was Here." *New York Review of Books* 22 Apr. 1971: 24–26.

Anderson, Susan Kay. " 'Freedom?' Richard Bautigan's First Wife, Virginia Aste, Speaks in a New Interview." *Arthur Magazine* 25 Dec. 2009. *Arthurmag.com.* Web. N. pag. 23 Feb. 2010.

Anon. "Books." *Playboy* 12 Mar. 1965: 22. *Archive.* Barber. Web. 1 Aug. 2007.

Barber, John F. *Richard Brautigan: An Annotated Bibliography.* Jefferson, NC: McFarland, 1990.

———, ed. *Brautigan Bibliography and Archive* (formerly *Richard Brautigan Bibliography and Archive*). Web. 25 July 2012.

———, ed. *Richard Brautigan: Essays on the Writings and Life.* Jefferson, NC: McFarland, 2007.

Barth, John. *The End of the Road.* 1958. Harmondsworth: Penguin, 1967.

———. *The Floating Opera.* 1956. Harmondsworth: Penguin, 1970.

———. *Giles Goat-Boy: or, The Revised New Syllabus.* 1966. Harmondsworth: Penguin, 1967.

———. "The Literature of Replenishment." 1980. *The Post-Modern Reader.* Ed. Charles Jenks. London: Academy Editions, 1992:

172–180.

——. *The Sot-Weed Factor*. 1960. London: Atlantic Books-Grove Atlantic, 2002.

Barthelme, Donald. *Snow White*. 1967. New York: Scribner Paperback, 1996.

Bashō, Matsuo. *Back Roads to Far Towns*. Trans. Cid Corman, and Kamaike Susumu. New York: Grossman, 1968.

Blackburn, Sara. "American Folk Hero." *Washington Post Book World* 28 Nov. 1971: 2. *Archive*. Barber. Web. 3 Jan. 2010.

Boyer, Jay. *Richard Brautigan*. Boise, Idaho: Boise State University Press c1987. Western Writers Series.

Brautigan, Ianthe. *You Can't Catch Death*. 2000. Edinburgh: Canongate, 2001.

Brautigan, Richard. *The Abortion: An Historical Romance 1966*. 1971. London: Picador-Pan, 1974.

——. *All Watched Over by Machines of Loving Grace*. San Francisco: The Communication Company, 1967.

——. *A Confederate General from Big Sur*. 1964. Edinburgh: Rebel Inc.-Canongate, 1999.

——. *Dreaming of Babylon: A Private Eye Novel 1942*. New York: Delacorte / Seymour Lawrence, 1977.

——. *The Edna Webster Collection of Undiscovered Writings*. New York: Mariner-Houghton Mifflin, 1999.

——. *The Galilee Hitch-Hiker*. San Francisco: White Rabbit Press, 1958.

——. *The Hawkline Monster: A Gothic Western*. 1974. London: Picador-Pan, 1976.

——. *I Watched the World Glide Effortlessly Bye and Other Pieces*. N. pag. Fairfax, CA: Burton Weiss and James P. Musser, 1996.

——. *In Watermelon Sugar*. 1968. London: Vintage, 2002.

———. *June 30ᵗʰ, June 30ᵗʰ*. New York: Delacorte / Seymour Lawrence, 1978.

———. *Lay the Marble Tea*. San Francisco: Carp, 1959.

———. *Loading Mercury with a Pitchfork*. New York: Simon and Schuster, 1976.

———. *The Octopus Frontier*. San Francisco: Carp, 1960.

———. "Old Lady." *The San Francisco Poets*. Meltzer: 293–294.

———. *The Pill* versus *the Springhill Mine Disaster*. 1968. In *Richard Brautigan's Trout Fishing* etc. By Brautigan.

———. *Please Plant This Book*. Santa Barbara, CA: Graham Mackintosh, 1968.

———. *The Return of the Rivers*. San Francisco: Inferno Press, 1957.

———. *Revenge of the Lawn: Stories 1962–1970*. 1971. Edinburgh: Canongate, 2006.

———. *Richard Brautigan's Trout Fishing in America, The Pill* versus *the Springhill Mine Disaster, and In Watermelon Sugar*. Boston: Houghton Mifflin / Seymour Lawrence, 1989.

———. *Rommel Drives on Deep into Egypt*. New York: Dell, 1970.

———. *So the Wind Won't Blow It All Away*. 1982. In *Richard Brautigan: Revenge of the Lawn, The Abortion, So the Wind Won't Blow It All Away*. New York: Houghton Mifflin / Seymour Lawrence, 1995.

———. *Sombrero Fallout: A Japanese Novel*. 1976. Edinburgh: Rebel Inc.-Canongate, 1998.

———. *The Tokyo-Montana Express*. 1979. New York: Delacorte / Seymour Lawrence, 1980.

———. *Trout Fishing in America*. San Francisco: Four Seasons Foundation, 1967.

———. ———. New York: Delta-Dell, 1969.

———.———. In *Richard Brautigan's Trout Fishing* etc. By Brautigan.

——. *An Unfortunate Woman*. 2000. Edinburgh: Rebel Inc.-Canongate, 2001.

——. *Willard and His Bowling Trophies: A Perverse Mystery*. 1975. London: Pan, 1977.

Burroughs, William S. *Junky*. 1953. London: Penguin, 1977.

——. *Naked Lunch*. 1959. *Naked Lunch: The Restored Text*. Eds. James Grauerholtz, and Barry Miles. London: Harper Perennial, 2005.

——. *Nova Express*. 1964. New York: Grove, 1992.

——. *The Soft Machine*. 1961. New York: Grove, 1992.

——. *The Ticket That Exploded*. 1962. London: Flamingo-HarperCollins, 2001.

Chénetier, Marc. *Richard Brautigan*. London: Methuen, 1983. Contemporary Writers Series.

Clark, William Bedford. "Abortion and the Missing Moral Center: Two Case Histories from the Post-Modern Novel." *Xavier Review* 4.1–2 (1984): 70–75.

Cook, Bruce. *The Beat Generation*. New York: Charles Scribner's Sons, 1971.

Coover, Robert. *The Origin of the Brunists*. 1966. St. Albans: Panther, 1968.

Corso, Gregory. *Gasoline and The Vestal Lady on Brattle*. *Vestal* 1955. San Francisco: City Lights, 1958. Pocket Poets Series 8.

Crane, Stephen. *The Red Badge of Courage*. 1895. Ed. Malcolm Bradbury. London: Everyman, 1993.

Culler, Jonathan. *Structuralist Poetics: Structuralism, Linguistics and the Study of Literature*. London: Routledge and Kegan Paul, 1975.

Dante. *The Divine Comedy, Vol. 1: Inferno*. Trans., introd., notes, commentary Mark Musa. New York: Penguin, 2003.

Davidson, Michael. *The San Francisco Renaissance: Poetics and Community at Mid-century.* 1989. Cambridge Studies in American Literature and Culture. Cambridge: Cambridge University Press, 1991. Davis, Kenn. "Sketches of Richard Brautigan." *Essays.* Barber: 65–87.

Deleuze, Gilles, and Félix Guattari. *Anti-Oedipus: Capitalism and Schizophrenia.* Trans. Robert Hurley, Mark Seem, and Helen R. Lane. London: Athlone, 1984.

Dietrich, Ronald F. "Brautigan's 'Homage to the San Francisco YMCA': A Modern Fairy Tale." *Notes on Contemporary Literature* 13.4 (1983): 2–4.

Eliot, T. S. "The Waste Land." 1922. *The Waste Land and Other Poems.* London: Faber and Faber, 1972: 23–41.

Ellingham, Lewis, and Kevin Killian. *Poet Be Like God: Jack Spicer and the San Francisco Renaissance.* Hanover, NH: University Press of New England, 1998.

Ellison, Ralph. *Invisible Man.* 1952. New York: Vintage International, 1995.

Federman, Raymond. *Double or Nothing: a Real Fictitious Discourse.* Chicago: Swallow Press, 1971.

Fiedler, Leslie. *Love and Death in the American Novel.* New York: Criterion Books, 1960.

Foster, Edward Halsey. *Richard Brautigan.* Boston: Twayne, c1983.

Gair, Christopher. *The American Counterculture.* Edinburgh: Edinburgh University Press, 2007.

——."'Perhaps the Words Remember Me': Richard Brautigan's Very Short Stories." *Western American Literature* 47.1 (Spring 2012): 5–21.

Gass, William H. *Omensetter's Luck.* 1966. London: Collins, 1967.

——.*Willie Masters' Lonesome Wife.* 1968. Normal, IL: Dalkey Archive Press, 1998.

Geyh, Paula, Fred G. Leebron, and Andrew Levy, eds. *Postmodern American Fiction: A Norton Anthology*. New York: Norton, 1998.

Ginsberg, Allen. *Howl and Other Poems.* Pocket Poets Series 4. San Francisco: City Lights, 1956.

Hackenberry, Charles. "Romance and Parody in Brautigan's *The Abortion*." *Critique: Studies in Modern Fiction* 23.2 (1982): 24–36.

Hearron, Thomas. "Escape through Imagination in *Trout Fishing in America*." *Critique: Studies in Modern Fiction* 16.1 (1974): 25–31.

Heilig, Steve. "Dreaming of Brautigan: An Appreciation." *Essays*. Barber: 121–124.

Hemingway, Ernest. *A Farewell to Arms*. 1929. London: Jonathan Cape, 1957.

——. *The First Forty-Nine Stories.* 1939. London: Arrow, 1993.

——. *In Our Time*. 1925. Included in *First Forty-Nine Stories*.

——. *The Sun Also Rises*. 1926. Published in UK as *Fiesta*. London: Jonathan Cape, 1927.

Hernlund, Patricia. "Author's Intent: *In Watermelon Sugar*." *Critique: Studies in Modern Fiction* 16.1 (1974): 5–17.

Hjortsberg, William. *Jubilee Hitchhiker: the life and times of Richard Brautigan.* Berkeley, CA: Counterpoint, 2012.

——. "Poetic Injustice? Maybe Richard Brautigan's Early Writings Did Not Deserve to See the Light of Day." *San Francisco Chronicle* 10 Oct. 1999: RV–3. *Archive*. Barber. Web. 10 Jan 2010.

Horvath, Brooke Kenton. "Richard Brautigan's Search for Control Over Death." *American Literature* 57.3 (1985): 434–455.

Hume, Kathryn. "Brautigan's Psychomachia." *Mosaic* 34.1 (2001): 75–92. *Highbeam.com*. Web. 27 Nov. 2009.

Jones, LeRoi. *The System of Dante's Hell*. New York: Grove, 1965.

Katz, Steve. *The Lestriad*. 1962. Flint, MI: Bamberger, 1987.

Kern, Robert. "Williams, Brautigan, and the Poetics of Primitivism." *Chicago Review* 27.1 (1975): 47–57.*Archive*. Barber. Web. 25 Feb. 2010.

Kerouac, Jack. *Big Sur*. 1962. London: Flamingo-HarperCollins, 2001.

——. *The Dharma Bums*. 1958. London: Penguin Classics, 2000.

——. *On the Road*. 1957. New York: Penguin, 1976.

Klinkowitz, Jerome. *The American 1960s: Imaginative Acts in a Decade of Change*. Ames, Iowa: Iowa State University Press, 1980.

——. *Literary Disruptions: The Making of a Post-Contemporary American Fiction*. Chicago: U of Illinois P, 1975.

Kosinski, Jerzy. *The Painted Bird*. New York: Houghton Mifflin, 1965.

Kramer, Jane. *Allen Ginsberg in America*. 1969. New York: Fromm, 1997.

Kyger, Joanne. "I Remember Richard Brautigan." *Essays*. Barber: 139–143.

Laing, R. D. *The Divided Self: an Existential Study in Sanity and Madness*. 1960. London: Penguin, 1969.

Langlois, Jim. "Brautigan, Richard." *Library Journal* 15 May 1971: 1726. *Archive*. Barber. Web. 12 Jan. 2010.

Leavitt, Harvey. "The Regained Paradise of Brautigan's *In Watermelon Sugar*." *Critique: Studies in Modern Fiction* 16.1 (1974): 18–24.

LeClair, Thomas. "The Art of Fiction No. 65." *Paris Review* Summer 1977. *Paris Review* website. 31 Oct. 2007.

Loewinsohn, Ron. "Preface: My Most Unforgettable Trout." *Trout Fishing in America*. San Francisco: Arion Press, 2003: xi–xxi. *Archive*. Barber. Web. 1 Feb. 2010.

Malley, Terence. *Richard Brautigan*. Writers for the Seventies. New York: Warner Paperback Library, 1972.

McClure, Michael. "Ninety–One Things About Richard Brautigan." *Essays*. Barber 162–187.

McDermott, James Dishon. *Austere Style in Twentieth-Century Literature: Literary Minimalism*. Lewiston, NY: Edwin Mellen, 2006.

Mellard, James M. *The Exploded Form: the Modernist Novel in America*. Chicago: U of Illinois P, 1980.

Meltzer, David, ed. *San Francisco Beat: Talking with the Poets*. San Francisco: City Lights, 2001.

——, ed. *The San Francisco Poets*. New York: Ballantine, 1971.

Mills, Joseph. *Reading Richard Brautigan's* Trout Fishing in America. Western Writers Series. Boise, Idaho: Boise State University Press, 1998.

O'Hara, Frank. "Personism: A Manifesto." 1959. *The Collected Poems of Frank O'Hara*. Ed. Donald Allen. Berkeley: University of California Press, 1995: 498–499.

Patchen, Kenneth. *The Journal of Albion Moonlight*. 1941. New York: Padell, 1946.

Perloff, Marjorie. *Frank O'Hara: Poet Among Painters*. New York: George Braziller, c1977.

Pütz, Manfred. "Transcendentalism Revived: the Fiction of Richard Brautigan." *Occident* 8 (1974): 39–47.

Pynchon, Thomas. *The Crying of Lot 49*. 1966. London: Vintage, 2000.

——. *V*. 1963. London: Pan, 1975.

Reed, Ishmael. *The Free-lance Pallbearers*. 1967. New York: Bantam, 1969.

Rexroth, Kenneth. *The Alternative Society: Essays from the Other World*. New York: Herder and Herder, 1972.

———. "Disengagement: the Art of the Beat Generation." 1957. *Alternative Society*: 1–16.

———, ed. and trans. *One Hundred Poems from the Japanese*. 1955. New York: New Directions, 1964.

Russell, Charles. "The Vault of Language: Self-Reflective Artifice in Contemporary American Fiction." *Modern Fiction Studies* 20.3 (1974): 349–359.

Schmitz, Neil. "Richard Brautigan and the Modern Pastoral." *Modern Fiction Studies* 19 Spring (1973): 109–125.

Schuyler, James. "Poet and Painter Overture." *The New American Poetry 1945–1960*. Ed. Donald Allen. New York: Grove Press, 1960: 418–419.

Seib, Kenneth. "*Trout Fishing in America*: Brautigan's Funky Fishing Yarn." *Critique: Studies in Modern Fiction* 13.2 (1971): 63–71.

Sorrentino, Gilbert. *The Sky Changes*. New York: Hill and Wang, 1966.

Spicer, Jack. *The Collected Books of Jack Spicer*. Ed. Robin Blaser. Los Angeles: Black Sparrow, 1975.

Tanner, Tony. *City of Words: American Fiction, 1950–1970*. London: Jonathan Cape, 1971.

———. "The Dream and the Pen." *The Times* 25 July 1970: 5.

———. *The Reign of Wonder: Naivety and Reality in American Literature*. Cambridge: Cambridge University Press, 1965.

Thoreau, Henry David. *Walden; or, Life in the Woods*. 1854. *Walden and Other Writings*. By Thoreau. Ed. Brooks Atkinson. New York: Modern Library-Random, 2000: 3–312.

Twain, Mark. *Adventures of Huckleberry Finn*. 1884. Harmondsworth: Puffin, 1953.

Ueda, Makoto, *Matsuo Bashō*. 1970. Trans. of Bashō by Ueda. Tokyo: Kodansha, 1982.

Vonnegut, Kurt. *Breakfast of Champions*. 1973. London: Vintage,

2000.

——. *Cat's Cradle*. 1963. London: Gollancz, 1971.

——. *God Bless You, Mr. Rosewater*. 1965. London: Vintage, 1992.

——. *Mother Night*. 1962. London: Vintage, 2000.

——. *Player Piano*. 1952. New York: Delta-Dell, 1999.

——. *The Sirens of Titan*. 1959. London: Gollancz, 2004.

——. *Slaughterhouse-Five*. 1969. London: Jonathan Cape, 1970.

Weiss, Burton. "Introduction." *I Watched the World Glide Effortlessly Bye and Other Pieces*. By Brautigan. N. pag.

Welch, Lew. "Brautigan's Moth Balanced on an Apple." *San Francisco Chronicle* 15 Dec. 1968: This World, 53, 59. *Archive*. Barber. Web. 13 Jan. 2010.

Wolfe, Tom. *The Electric Kool-Aid Acid Test*. 1968. New York: Bantam, 1999.

——. "The New Journalism." *The New Journalism*. Eds. Wolfe, and E. W. Johnson. 1973. London: Picador, 1996: 15–68.

Wright, Lawrence. "The Life and Death of Richard Brautigan." *Rolling Stone* 11 Apr. 1985: 29+. *Archive*. Barber. Web. 8 Jan. 2010.

A Note on the Author

John Tanner was born in South Wales, graduated from Swansea University, and worked as a journalist on regional and national newspapers before becoming a corporate executive with a publishing group. He took advantage of early retirement in 2001 to pursue a radically different course, as a poet and academic. He chose to write his doctoral thesis on Brautigan after coming across *Trout Fishing in America* in a second-hand book shop in Arizona. "It's not about how to fish," the shop assistant warned him.

He now teaches English Literature and Creative Writing at Bangor University. He has presented several papers on Brautigan and has written the entry for him in the online resource, *The Literary Encyclopaedia*. He is an elected member of the Welsh Academy of writers and his poetry has appeared in various magazines, in the anthology *The Lie of the Land*, and in the collected volume of his verse, *Pieces*, both published by Cinnamon Press. He lives in North Wales.

Humanities-Ebooks.co.uk

All Humanities Ebooks titles are available to Libraries through Ebrary, EBSCO and Ingram Digital (MyiLibrary.com)

Some Academic titles

Sibylle Baumbach, *Shakespeare and the Art of Physiognomy*
John Beer, *Blake's Humanism*
John Beer, *The Achievement of E M Forster*
John Beer, *Coleridge the Visionary*
Jared Curtis, ed., *The Fenwick Notes of William Wordsworth**
Jared Curtis, ed., *The Cornell Wordsworth: A Supplement**
Steven Duncan, *Analytic Philosophy of Religion: its History since 1955**
John K Hale, *Milton as Multilingual: Selected Essays 1982–2004*
Simon Hull, ed., *The British Periodical Text, 1797–1835*
Rob Johnson, Mark Levene and Penny Roberts, eds., *History at the End of the World* *
John Lennard, *Modern Dragons and other Essays on Genre Fiction**
C W R D Moseley, *Shakespeare's History Plays*
Paul McDonald, *Laughing at the Darkness: Postmodernism and American Humour* *
Colin Nicholson, *Fivefathers: Interviews with late Twentieth-Century Scottish Poets*
W J B Owen, *Understanding 'The Prelude'*
Pamela Perkins, ed., *Francis Jeffrey's Highland and Continental Tours**
Keith Sagar, *D. H. Lawrence: Poet**
Reinaldo Francisco Silva, *Portuguese American Literature**
Trudi Tate, *Modernism History and the First World War**
William Wordsworth, *Concerning the Convention of Cintra**
W J B Owen and J W Smyser, eds., *Wordsworth's Political Writings**
The Poems of William Wordsworth: Collected Reading Texts from the Cornell Wordsworth, 3 vols.*

* These titles are also available in print using links from
http://www.humanities-ebooks.co.uk

Humanities Insights

These are some of the Insights available at:
http://www.humanities-ebooks.co.uk/

General Titles

An Introduction to Critical Theory
Modern Feminist Theory
An Introduction to Rhetorical Terms

Genre FictionSightlines

Octavia E Butler: *Xenogenesis / Lilith's Brood*
Reginal Hill: *On Beulah's Height*
Ian McDonald: *Chaga / Evolution's Store*
Walter Mosley: *Devil in a Blue Dress*
Tamora Pierce: *The Immortals*

History Insights

Oliver Cromwell
The British Empire: Pomp, Power and Postcolonialism
The Holocaust: Events, Motives, Legacy
Lenin's Revolution
Methodism and Society
The Risorgimento

Literature Insights

Austen: *Emma*
Conrad: *The Secret Agent*
Eliot, T S: 'The Love Song of J Alfred Prufrock' and *The Waste Land*
English Renaissance Drama: Theatre and Theatres in Shakespeare's Time
Reading William Faulkner: *Go Down, Moses* and *Big Woods'*
Faulkner: *The Sound and the Fury*
Gaskell, *Mary Barton*
Hardy: *Tess of the Durbervilles*
Ibsen: *The Doll's House*
Hopkins: Selected Poems
Ted Hughes: *New Selected Poems*
Philip Larkin: *Selected Poems*
Lawrence: Selected Short Stories
Lawrence: *Sons and Lovers*
Lawrence: *Women in Love*
Paul Scott: *The Raj Quartet*

Shakespeare: *Hamlet*
Shakespeare: *Henry IV*
Shakespeare: *King Lear*
Shakespeare: *Richard II*
Shakespeare: *Richard III*
Shakespeare: *The Merchant of Venice*
Shakespeare: *The Tempest*
Shakespeare: *Troilus and Cressida*
Shelley: *Frankenstein*
Wordsworth: *Lyrical Ballads*
Fields of Agony: English Poetry and the First World War

Philosophy Insights

American Pragmatism
Barthes
Thinking Ethically about Business
Critical Thinking
Existentialism
Formal Logic
Metaethics
Contemporary Philosophy of Religion
Philosophy of Sport
Plato
Wittgenstein
Žižek

Some Titles in Preparation

Aesthetics
Philosophy of Language
Philosophy of Mind
Political Psychology
Plato's *Republic*
Renaissance Philosophy
Rousseau's legacy

Austen: *Pride and Prejudice*
Blake: *Songs of Innocence & Experience*
Chatwin: *In Patagonia*
Dreiser: *Sister Carrie*
Eliot, George: *Silas Marner*
Eliot: *Four Quartets*
Fitzgerald: *The Great Gatsby*
Hardy: Selected Poems
Heaney: Selected Poems
James: *The Ambassadors*
Lawrence: *The Rainbow*
Melville: *Moby-Dick*
Melville: Three Novellas
Shakespeare: *Macbeth*
Shakespeare: *Romeo and Juliet*